E=mc²

ESCAPE INTO RELATIVITY

ANDRZEJ ZALEWSKI

Ordering Information:

Books to Life Marketing Ltd
70 Coulson's Road, Bristol BS14 0NW, UK

Printed in the United States of America

CHAPTER 1

The helicopter UH-60A Black hawk slowly was approaching to its destination. It was night. The machine flew over the Golden Gate Bridge and had made huge bend above the waters of Bay of San Francisco. It had on the board the crew and three passengers. Among them, there was one distinctive man and two marines escorting this one. He was dressed in raincoat and wore the cap. This one detail distinguished him from two of them, because it was a cap of admiral. Yes, he was a admiral. He had long face and was dark-haired man, wearing this cap on his head. Now the helicopter had flown high over the bridge and was approaching to the port if San Francisco. It was closer and closer its destination, and passing on the left the island named "Rock". The island is famous from the cause, on it is the prison named "Alcatraz". Now it is the museum, from the nineteen sixty third year. Lighted right now. Because of the night. So, admiral could see it through the window of machine. Later they flew near the Treasure Island, they had it also on the left side, and over the big bridge, it was lighted, illuminated at this moment and after that they were nearer their place of landing. It took certain moment when they were over the pier eighty. It was their destination. The helicopter slowly began to approach to this place. Pilot reduced the highness and smoothly landed on the ground. When the machine touched the earth, making the dust around, admiral felt the, landing was over. In the distance, from the place of landing, there, stood a little group of people waiting until the manoeuvre has been done. The admiral put aside the safety belt, and went out of the machine. When his foot felt the concrete, he became more confident about his situation.

After that went out the two marines. The dust was still in the air, and they quickly went out the range of helicopter. From the waiting group separated one man, dressed in uniform of commodore. He approached to the admiral and they shook hands. The commodore overcoming the noise of helicopter said to admiral.

"Nice to see you, sir!"

The admiral looked on him, sternly, and asked commodore.

"Why were you calling me?"

"It is very grave matter, I have to you," answered commodore, "I want to show you something. When you will see, you will understand everything."

So, they went together from the place of landing of the helicopter to the near hangar. It was opened and admiral in the light of lamppost could see the entrance to this hangar. When they were together inside it, he saw many things placed there, but commodore did not stopped at them, only went foward to the certain part of this hangar. There, stood on the wooden elements some kind of pack, from one side opened and visible, what is inside, and commodore showed it for the admiral, to look. Admiral approached and saw one thing. It was looking like big iron ball, and had on one part of it the information plate…when admiral read it, his legs became like rubber…he felt faintly himself. On the small plate has been written "Golden Fleece Machine." He swallowed the saliva and looked on commodore. This one was, also, upset and did not know what to do, at this moment. On their faces, now, has been seen, they have a big problem. Huge problem. And they needed to resolve that one. Surely.

"It is not everything," said commodore, "we have Silva," he added and saw it made a big impression on the admiral. This one looked on commodore more surprised than before.

"Could you explain it more precisely?"

"One of the ship berthed to this pier, and when they wanted to unload, on the deck of this ship he appeared, you know, he wanted to gulp a fresh air, and one of the zworker of port noticed him and recognized. And after that called to police. That is all. We keep him in the bureau of pier eighty. I will lead you to him," slowly said commodore. Of course the bureau has been build in recent time.

After that they went out of this hangar and directed to the building where was the office of this pier. When they were walking to this bureau commodor was beginning to explain the situation farther.

"I did not interrogated him until now. We were waiting for you, because you know in this matter most than we. I must tell, except me, there inside, are the agents of FBI. You were the head of government commission, and I thought it will be better to wait for your arrival."

For the first moment admiral had pretension to the commodore, why he disturbed his quiet and peacefull life, but now he understand everything. His presence at the interrogation of Silva was obvious. So, he must be here and conduct the whole affair. And now were trying to collect the thoughts how to lead this matter farther. It was his case, event in his life, crucial moment. And now everything began again. As several years ago. They were on the trail of this matter. When the admiral was considering all circumstances refer to this matter, he was sure, it will not be easy. At this moment they, together were stepping toward the compound of building, where was kept the Silva. After several minutes they were at the place, in the room where was Silva and three agents of FBI. They have been keeping Silva, controlling him, and waited for commodore. Silva was looked tired and exhausted sitting on a chair at the table. Around him stood three agents of FBI. The room was slightly lit, and had not enough furniture, only this one table and two chair, on which one of them was sitting Silva. Admiral looked on him sternly. They are meeting together once again, after several years of not seeing each other. Silva had rather regrettable look. His appearance was like drunk man. When admiral came in, he looked on him with surprise and did not hide it. Now he felt himself more worried than before. He was like little kid waiting for punishment. But there was no anyone who could help him.

"Good morning Mr. Silva. We are meeting again. Sorry, if it is inconvenient for you...," at this moment the admiral broke the speech to Silva, because commodore needed to introduce for him the rest of persons, present in the room.

"Mr. admiral, may I introduce you the agents of FBI?" and after a short moment, he pointed on each of them, "this is John Snowden, Alfred Grisham and Aaron Rehab," after the introduction, they were shaking hands with admiral and went farther to the essence of the matter.

"We are waiting for you already several hours. Mr. commodore has said, you must be present at this affair, because you were at this matter in former time, from the government side. And you are the most adequate person in the whole case," Snowden said slowly, "you must be present in our investigation. Mr. Silva is wanted by the law. When we caught him, we have learned that Mr. Kozinsky, commodore is connected with the matter. So, we have been looking for him, as you see, with success, and informed him about whole case, and he arrived here. That is all."

At this moment Kozinsky, the commodore again broke the speech of Snowden and said:

"Mr. Admiral don't be angry, I invite you here, please, you understand, why I did called for you," commodore said to admiral.

This one nodded wholly agreeing with that decision. After these explanation he looked on Silva and started out again the conversation with him…

"Mr. Silva, you are conscious about the whole affair, in which you are now. You must be fully co-operative with us, if not we will use others methods, to know all about you. I must mention, your situation is very bad. Tell me everything, what you were doing after resolving the "Golden Fleece" group?"

Silva only looked on admiral with dull sight and moving slightly on a chair, did not say any word. Who could have predicted about whole affair. Now they all were waiting, what he will say, but Silva was silent. Admiral waiting a moment, but seeing his words did not make any impression on Silva, he said stronger than before:

"You are sought by the whole jurisdiction of the world! Mr. Silva!" this time admiral said it loudly. "If you will not say for me about you past time, what you were doing, during this all several years, you will have big trouble. So, it is in your interest to explain what we need. We will help you in the farther process." Admiral was looking for-in his mind, the other ways, how to press Silva and make him to the co-operation with them. He decided to be more firm and don't give for Silva any occasion to repose. And than, when they used such strategy it brought the effect. Silva for the first time felt anxiety and became nervous, so, he moved on a chair uncertain and it was noticed by his tormentors, as he thought about the admiral, commodore and agents. He wanted to calm at this moment, but it was difficult and he could not find the way, how to achieve it. Yes, he was under pressure. The admiral, and others, present in this room were looking on him with disregard and wanted get whole information about him. But, he was still silent and did not give any of it. Many could believe he is mute, because he did not say any word for them, even through the whole time, to the moment, the admiral's arrival. But, of course it was wrong. He wanted only get some kind of guarantee, in the near future, for example at the court, so it was the cause of his silence. Admiral took second chair, has sat at the table and looking deeply in the eyes of Silva, said:

"We are listening Mr. Silva. We are all ears."

Patrick Silva-it was his full name, moved a little, swallow saliva, and slowly said to the admiral.

"What can you guarantee for me? If I tell you everything."

"It depends. What you will say," answered admiral.

"I... I had a troubles...," for the first time Silva considered his own situation, and thought, it will be better to co-operate with them, so he said these several words. At this moment interfered Snowden.

"Mr. admiral. I think better will be to continue our interrogation at the headquarters of FBI, here in our town. At the "White House".

Admiral looked on him a little confused, but agreed for such proposal. Snowden had right. This place, at which they were now wasn't proper for this kind of matter. So, they must go to the center of FBI here in San Francisco, placed at the Golden Gate Avenue. It was called the "White House" for the reason of white colour of the building. Commodore gave a sign for Silva to go. They even not handcuffed him only took his body under arms and went out the room. After that, they all were in corridor still keeping Silva strongly, because they felt he was weak and shambling on his legs. It took several minutes when they were outside the building. They came to the autos and pushed him inside one of the cars. He sat down heavily on backseat deeply gasping for breath. Snowden took the place of driver and rest of the company to the second car. Of course Silva was kept by one of the agents. They lit the engines of their cars and whole group rode out the space of pier eighty. Soon, they were on the Cesar Chavez Street. And then, they turned on the left to Kansas Street, passed it and found on the Marin Street. Turned on the right, it was short way leading them to the one hundred and one number of motorway, and they needed to turn on the right to the drive which is connection with the motorway. So, after a moment they were on the one hundred and one. Snowden was on the front and accelerating a little felt relief, they were after the first moment of whole matter. And the rest of company after him. He knew the way as his own pocket, so, it was not difficult for him to go, to drive to the headquarters of FBI. Many years of service as a cop in San Francisco area has been learned him profoundly about this town. He was experienced agent, and had many success in his work. And now-he thought, will be the same. But he did not know, this case had bigger range than he could expect. He supposed, he will be drive this investigation, but it has been misleading what he thought. And he did not know the history of the whole story. Moreover the presence of admiral and commodore was intriguing him.

"Why? Why are they here?" passing through his mind. He could not understand. He had only information, Silva is wanted by the police. And nothing more. And the order to find the commodore, if such matter will appear. So, he did what was needed. That is all. And now they were driving the motorway to the center of San Francisco. They passed on the right the Potrero Hill and was near the junction which is leading to the Market Street. He now was riding more slowly, because they were closer the Van Ness Avenue. It is the crossroads with Market Street. An after passing it the motorway one hundred and one is called the Van Ness avenue and is leading to the Golden Gate Bridge. So they rode this way farther, until they had on the right the Golden Gate Avenue. They turned to this one, rode this way and found at the headquarters of FBI, the "White House" building as it is named in such a way. After a moment they have parked their cars on the left side of the Avenue. And the journey was over. They all sat out the cars and went to the entrance of this building. Soon, whole group was in the room where the investigation can be make. Now Patrick Silva was sitting at the table, nervously rubbing his hands. He wanted to rest, repose, desired it so much, but of course it was not possible. The whole conversation with him was recording so, the agents could present it in the court. First of them spoke the admiral:

"Mr. Silva can you co-operate with us? Have you desire to do it?"

He nodded agreeing with admiral, because he knew they will learn about everything from the two men, which were with him. They joined the crew of the ship at the last moment, when the ship was beginning the voyage through Pacific. The police kept control over that ship and the papers of it right now. And FBI will know about last port from which they started the swim. Silva has deprived any illusion concerning his person. Now, he knew his position was bad. And he knew they will know all about him and the whole matter, in which he was. He wanted only to rest. Repose. After several seconds he began to speak.

"Sir, I… I had some problem. After the resolving the group of scientists of the project" Golden Fleece" I hadn't the job. I was looking for it, but without any result. And moreover began to game. In Las Vegas. I needed money. And soon fell in debts. They were rising, but I hadn't the cash to pay. So, I was in troubles. You can't believe, but it is truth. And after a several days in my hotel room appeared two men…, "he, at this moment hesitated a little and looked on admiral, but this one hadn't mercy and looked stern on Silva.

"They offered for you the help?" he said.

"Yes. You guessed, "answered Silva," they said, they will pay all my debts, but they wanted me. If I will not meet all their conditions they will give whole matter to the court. So, what could I do? At that moment it was good for me, and they offered me job. To work for them."

"You still have been going to work at the project "Golden Fleece?"

The admiral looked on Silva with disgust. Slowly the parts of this puzzle became more concrete. He wanted to know who is staying behind the affair. It was crucial fact and he wanted, Silva will give him more concrete information about this matter, so he did not give him occasion to rest. That was his method to lead the interrogation. The rest of company, namely the agents and commodore gave him priority to make it. This was difficult time for everyone, to achieve a success in their work, and they did not disturb for him to make it. Kozinsky, the commodore, knew, the admiral was the proper person in this matter. He knew more than the rest. So, they did not interrupt for him to do it. By the way, he was the head of commission from the givernment side to keep control over their research in the former time. The interrogation has been going, and at that time, the three agents of their group got the call from the director of this post of FBI. He wanted to see them, right now in his cabinet. And they according to the order went out the room of investigation and were going to him. Soon, they found in his study. He showed them to rest and began ask, how the matter is going.

"You know, I agreed on the case, it can be make in our court-yard, but we keep this man not according to the law. And the rest of this company. We need to give opportunity for them to meet with the lawyer. Can you give me the information how the matter is going?" the director asked them.

First answered Snowden.

"For me it is like… absurd. This man, Silva, is talking always about the theory of relativity. Something like Einstein and every-thing about him."

"Yes, he talks only about it," interrupted other agent.

"Can you know, from what place arrived this ship?"

"From Bali."

"What?"

"From Bali," repeated the same agent, and added. "From Indonesia."

For the director it was enough. So, he understood everything. The matter was beyond his competence.

"But, why the load is on our territory?" he asked.

"We don't know. Maybe in the future we will know about all facts, concerning this matter," answered Snowden.

"We need get rid of them, as quickly as possible." Ended director. "Go to them and give our help, okay?"

The three agents rose from the seats and left the director with his own thoughts. He, now had a problem with this case and must manage with this one. For him it was enough troubles with many others cases, and this matter added more difficult fact to resolve it. He hadn't humour at that moment. All was strange for him and he did not understand what is going on in this whole affair. It was beyond his idea.

"What are they looking for?" passed through his mind. Now, he had more confusion about whole matter and wanted get rid of it. And who will prepare the paper work concerning this one? So, he decided to give it for one of the agents.

"We need peace here," was his conclusion.

At the same time admiral and commodore tormented Silva wanting to get all information about the activity of him. About last years, after his disappearance. He was tired and wanted to rest. Repose. So, piece by piece he gave them the account of his life. Slowly, by turns revvealed the details of secret of the "Golden Fleece" project. For Ford-it was the name of admiral, was enough act farther. He knew all fact concerning these things. Namely the "Golden Fleece" project. He looked on Kozinsky and said:

"The matter is very serious. We need to act quickly. I must inform about all fact the Washington, even the President, but how can I do it?"

"Maybe you know somebody who can help?" was the answer of commodore.

"Yes…you have right. I'm thinking about one person…"

At this moment, went in the room the three agents. After the conversation with the director.

"Have you any progress?" asked one of them.

"We have all what we need," answered admiral.

"I have asked you, because…you know, we must act according to the law. The situation is very inconvenient for us. We keep them, and not giving the opportunity to meet with the lawyer," continued the agent. "It is against the rule…"

"I will prepare everything. Don't worry," said Ford, "only give us time to do it."

The three agents became calm after such words.

"What you decided?"

"I must inform the Washington about whole matter, that is all."

After such answer these three didn't ask more question. They understood it was far beyond their competence.

"We will help you, as we can," again said the same agent. The two of them nodded agreeing with him.

The admiral took from his pocket the smartphone after such words and said to the commodore:

"I'm thinking about one man. Namely the Vice-President of previous government. Even if he is from the opposite party. He told me, I can call to him at every moment and in any case. So this is very important, and I think he will help for us to contact with the "White House". I have his number."

Kozinsky looked on him, smiling a little. At the same time Silva was holding his hands on the table and making sad view. His head was dropped, the hair in mess and was sitting quietly without any move. But now nobody was looking on him. They were absorbing what was doing the admiral. He kept the telephone in his hand at the ear and waited, until someone will answer on the signal. But without any result.

"I will call later," he said disappointed.

Commodore was also in such mood.

"What do we now?" he asked

"Don't worry, I will do it again after certain time. Surely he is occupied right now, but I know he will help for us," after these words he turned to the agents and said, "please keep this man farther. We need to wait for the contact with the Vice-President. I think it is best way to resolve our problem,"

They agreed with him. Whole affair was difficult, and without the help of the government it can't be resolved. Snowden, now was content, he will not be at that matter. He had enough others problem also not ended and he felt the relief it will be in the hands of this admiral and commodore. He, like the others too needed the rest and refresh. To change the clothes, take the shower, and then occupy with the work. The rest of the company needed the same. They were tired and close this affair as quickly as possible. They desired it. The whole case was inconvenient for this three agents, and their boss wanted to get rid of it. And than they will have, in the future, the problem behind. The matter belongs to Ford and Kozinsky. The FBI here, in San Francisco wasn't proper institution to occupy with such case. To manage with it. So, in that way passed a few minutes, and again the admiral took attempt to call to the Vice-President. He held the telephone at the head and waited for result. Through several seconds there was not answer, but after certain time someone said in the loudspeaker. And than the connection was possible. Admiral approached to the corner of the room detached himself from the group and began to speak. His voice was loud, because he wanted to be audible by this person, on the other side of linkage. He threw a few words of greetings to the telephone. He was heard by his interlocutor. Ford has begun his conversation with the ex-Vice-President and the group in this room heard a little it. They now concentrated on the result of this talking. After a moment the face of Ford became light, and he smiled a little showing, the conversation was positive. It took a several minutes, and admiral with joyful visage ended his speaking. He turned to them and revealed his secret talking. It was obvious he had success. The ex-Vice-President took the matter in his hands Even, if he had been from opposite camp, the state duty needed to be fulfilled by every state worker. Now they had contact with the White House, and for them stayed only to wait for the message and instruction from the Washington. Everything seems to be on best way.

"They will keep contact with you. Do you understand?" admiral said it slowly. "But now I and commodore need to rest. Which hotel will you recommend?"

"I recommend the Nikko," said Snowden, "Nikko means sun light in Japanese language."

"So, let's go,"

After saying this they went out the room and found on the street at the car. Soon they were riding the Golden Gate Avenue to the hotel. They passed Hyde street on the left, and next was Leaven Worth street in which they turned and after a moment were on the O'Farrell street and there was the hotel "Nikko". The entrance to this one was from this street. Snowden parked the auto on the right side of the street. He stopped and admiral and commodore got off, then went to the entrance. When they were inside, there was cold and the air-conditioning was kept. After several meters they turned on the right and went up the few steps and found in big lobby. On the left there was reception and Kozinsky approached to it settle their staying in this hotel. So, after certain time they together went to the elevators and stayed there for a moment waiting for one of it. The place was nicely arranged, on the walls the were the mirror in which they saw their own silhouettes. It took-the waiting several seconds. Yes, it was the Japanese precision, the Mitsubishy work, so, when the door has opened they went inside the cabin. Kozinsky pressed the button of twenty first floor, and did not even felt when the elevator was going up. It was only a moment when they were on this floor. The door has opened and they were on the right, proper corridor. Only for them left to look for their rooms. With the magnetic card inserted in the slot of the door, the lock was opened and Kozinsky went to the inside of his room. The same made the admiral. The rooms were well prepared and were nice. Silent and quiet. In the room of admiral was one bed, and he put his cap on it. Then he made the same with his raincoat. The on the wall was fixed the tv set, but he did not turn ot on, only wanted to take the shower. Undressed went to the bath-room. Yes, this time it was nice. Very nice. He made the washing a lot, relishing at the same time. "Maybe the commodore is making the same," went through his mind. He smiled a little, when he thought about the price of their luxury.

"We can effort it. The firm will pay," passed through his mind, and he was using it with pleasure. This enjoyment took even half an hour, washing-up not only the dirtinesss, but also the unpleasant moments of the last events. So, refreshed, took the towel and wound his body with it laid on the bed and began think about these events of the past.

"What we can do now?" he asked himself, but could not imagine any scenario what will be in the future. He looked on his wristwatch and saw the digits. It was early time. After a moment he heard the knocking to the door. Got up and approached to it, and then opened. There on the corridor stood the commodore. He was cleanly and wanted to be with admiral.

"Can I come in?" he asked.

"Yes, Sure," answered Ford.

"It is very rude to stay behind the wall and not say any word with you," continued Kozinsky, "so, I thought will be better to talk with you."

"Sorry, for my dress, I took the shower."

"I did the same but I was in time to dress."

"Please come in." Ford encouraged him.

After several minutes commodore began the conversation again.

"Maybe we will take the dinner?" he proposed.

Admiral agreed with him so, he took the receiver and order several dishes also, of course, with the suchi. They waited several minutes for arrival of the worker of hotel. He went in and put the dishes on the small table. Admiral smilled a little, when he thought about the meal. In the meantime he dressed himself and then sat behind the table. They ate in silence and did not talk. After finishing it Ford turned on the tv. Immediately appeared the picture on the screen. He and commodore saw the two men and heard the dialogue between them. Through the moment they did not pay attention to the conversation, but after a while to their ears came something interesting and they heard it was about the theory of relativity. They stopped to speak and turned to the tv set, concentrated on the programm. In the vision, there, on the screen were two men talking each other. It was science programm. And it was obvious, one of the men was scientist. The second, the reporter, and he was asking this scientist just about the theory.

"Could you explain the uncertainty principle of Heinserberg?" was the voice of reporter.

"Sure. It is named after Werner Karl Heinserberg. He formulated such principle. For me it is, like the theory of relativity, as simple as the straight wire, "answered the scientist.

"Could you explain it profoundly?"

"It defines the information about the examined particle of matter. When we wanted to get the information about it, we use certain length of wave. And when we want to know something about such particle, if it is smaller we are using smaller leangth of wave and automatically we get smaller amount of information about this particle."

"Could explain in simplle words the theory of relativity?"

"It is discovered by Einstein. When he worked in patent office as a young man. It is divided on two parts. The general and particular. But, if we want to understand it, I must say what it is. When we have a paradox it is looking for the explanation of it. To find the main object in dilema. To find the truth in certain problem. That is all. Which part of paradox is the truth. And that is, why it is named the theory of relativity. Correctly saying, where is the point to which we could relate."

"Yes, it is simple."

"But, moreover I must say that many scientist believe, that according to this theory we have, for example bad rule to which are built our computers."

"It is interesting. Do you want to say, we have bad computers?'

"Yes. Exactly. The human being is not thinking in the way as our computers are thinking."

"It is incredible. Do you want to say, we have scrap?"

"That is correct," said this scientist.

"Where is the fault, the mistake?"

"I don't know, but they give the example. The computer is thinking by the byte, and they, the scientists give the presumption that man is thinking by three elements, not by two."

"It is like eureka! Do you think, that is truth?"

"I don't know, but, there is something intriguing in that fact,"

Admiral and commodore were looking on the tv screen and were astonished. They did not presumed, there, in the world were so much information on the subject concerning the theory of relativity.

This one man, the scientist surely must know more than they can predict. And they looked on the screen with misgiving, their secret is discovered by other group of scientists. What to do now? Who could have predicted that it will repeat again?

"We have big problem," admiral said to Kozinsky.

This one looked on him seriously and asked a question:

"What the Vice-President said to you?

"He said, everything will be prepared. Someone will arrive to us from Washington. Surely, he has more possibility to go, to the "'White House", than me. For me, I would like stay here and not go to the headquarters of FBI. It is bigger pleasure to wait for them here than over there. Do you agree?"

"You said exactly what I need, also." Answered Kozinsky.

The programm on the screen ended and after that appeared the publicity. So, they did not pay attention what was going on, on the screen, only wanted to stay in this room together waiting for the next hours and arrival of the men from Washington. The time went quickly, and they didn't even notice there was the middle of the day. In the meantime the admiral dressed himself, and said to Kozinsky he wanted to sleep. Even several hours. So, commodore left him and went to his own room, and after a moment did the same. It was very tiring day and of course they needed a repose. Such facts weren't so important, only was needed to mention they had nice dreams.

CHAPTER 2

"Welcome you from Madison Square Garden. My name is William Luedke. And I want to invite you from this venue to take part in today event. We have the performance of Hanna O'Hara. And I think you will be satisfied to sacrifice several hours to this one. She, now again returned on the stage after long absence caused by her illness. But now she will be before us, and will perform for us showing her talent as a singer knowing worldwide. We have hope that even now it will be very amazing and charming, and as I have said it will satisfy us profoundly. Until now she had the illness, but she returned to the health, and I have hope she will give for us splendid show. So, we are transmitting this event at this moment fully convinced that even now it will be worth to see it. She is famous around the world, and keeps the spectators in the great admiration. So, for me stayed to invite you to today evening and relish from the great show." The reporter had said to the camera held by camera man. Then the action was carried to the inside, where was the scene in center of auditorium. It was placed in the middle like it had been made in nineteen seventy-fourth year. When Frank Sinatra has been performing. It was prepared in the same way. But this time over the scene were the huge screens of TV, than it was in former time when were the reflectors placed there. The audience was waiting with iimpatience for her demonstration. In near distance to the scene was seating Margaret with her husband, and they also were waiting for the show. Margaret was nice dressed in the black gown and in addition was wearing the jewellery. All her silhouette was beautiful and looking proper to this evening. She was nice and very proud for her husband. Lambert had many reasons to pride that he had such woman. She was pretty and young. Yes, it was the cause why he was happy to have such splendid woman. He looked on her and saw, this time she was content to be here in such evening and at this place. For this moment they are waiting, until Hanna O'Hara will appear on the stage. They kept their guides with the program of that event and were a little impatient for her arrive. And soon, the artist had appeared. The show just began. Hanna O'Hara was the singer and all he shows always was great events. She had a talent and had showed, every of her performances had given splendid joy for the spectators. And this time it was the same. Every time it was success. After a while when she sang her best song, the audience was in the best admiration. For her art and talent. They were astonished and expressed their amazement with huge applause. Margaret made the same, and the show was continued. Hanna O'Hara was best artist and gave the most great performaance before the audience. This evening was fulfilled with joy profoundly. Everyone had satisfaction. It wasn't time waste. So, the evening was passing quickly and the hours of the show came to the the end. Hanna O'Hara was called fot repeat it again by spectators, and she gave to more songs for them. All were satisfied, and after that people began to go out from the hall. But Margaret and her husband decided to stay, until will be possible walk out without any problem. When will be rarely. They both stayed on their place waiting for this moment, and didn't move from it. Yes, it was nice evening. Lambert's wife was content, and when they were standing on the place, to them suddenly approached certain person, also, dressed in suit as Lambert.

"Excuse me sir…" this one had said, coming from the back of the couple.

Lambert turned and saw his subordinate, Frank Green, and was surprised to see him here.

"Oh?! It is you…what are you doing here?" asked Lambert.

"We have a problem sir," answered Green.

"Is it important?"

"Yes, very important," said his subordinate.

"Could you wait to tell me this tomorrow? Could not waiting with it until my return to the bureau?" Lambert was irritable.

"No, sir I can't," again answered Green.

"So, what you want?" at last agreed Lambert.

"We have a problem with "Golden Fleece" sir ."

For this moment Lambert looked on him not so nice as before. The smile disappeared from the face of boss. This good knowing sound of this word "Golden Fleece" was too important to ignore it right now, even at this nice moment.

"What is happening?" he asked.

"I have not connection with our man in San Francisco,"

For such answer Lambert stood and seemed to look somewhere before him without any aim. So, standing in the same place without any word, he waited there through a moment till he said:

"Let's go to the office," he decided. And then said to his wife, "my dear you must go home without me. Boys will go with you escorting you together. I have some problem, and I need to occupy with it. It is very important for me."

His wife was not joyful for such proposition and it was visible on her face. She knew, her husband had and has always the truth, and better will be to adopt to his counsel. And after that they separated each other, so, Lambert went with Green to his car in the garage of Madison Square Garden. Soon they were on Broadway and were riding to the Lower Manhattan, and there stands their skyscraper. Huge building with fifty five floors. When they approached to this one, there was free space for parking the cars before this building. They went out the car after their arrival to this place, and went directly to the entrance of the skyscrape. They have gone through the glass door and were in huge lobby where was the post of guard. For the first moment the guy did not notice them. He had the monitoring. The huge screen of vision, of the cameras, but did not observed it and was absorbing, reading the newspaper. Lambert has seen this, but did not tell off him for such negligence of duty. At the post of guard was the barrier, and if someone would wanted to go farther he had to go through this barrier. Immediately the guard, when he noticed Lambert and Green pressed the button and opened the way for them.

The bar was removed and they went through it. Next they went to the place where were the standings of elevators. They acted quickly. Green pressed on of the button on the wall, and pull down one of the elevators. The door has been opening and they went to the inside of the cabin. When they were in it, Green again pressed the one of the buttons of the cabin, namely the fifty fourth floor. The cabin budged and began the ride. Soon they were on the needed floor, but the study of Lambert was on the fifty fifth floor. When Lambert wanted to go to this floor he needed to use special kind of key and insert it in the proper slot placed in this cabin. And then the elevator was pulled up of one floor more. Above. It was made for the security reason. So, Lambert took from the pocket behind the suit lapel some kind of magnetic card, inserted it in this slot and the cabin again budged and was pulled higher. And after that the door was opened. on one floor more. They went out of the cabin and found in certain corridor. On the walls of it could be seen many souvenirs. The whole life of Lambert. It was history of "Lambert Industry". That was the name of his concern. So, they went several steps and found in his study. He put his raincoat on the one of the leather armchairs and approached to the small table where were the bottles with alcohol. He took the glass and poured a little gin in. At last he said to Green. He the whole way was silent.

"So, relate me what you know,"

Green had one moment of hesitancy, but after that he answered.

"I called to our man in San Francisco several times but hadn't connection."

"So, is it the reason for disturb my pleasure?" again said Lambert.

"I think, we must keep control in whole time," slowly said Green.

"I think you make the storm in the glass. You had always tendency to exaggerate the all things."

"I wanted only to inform you about that fact. Better will be to call again and to know exactly what is going now. Do you agree?"

"Yes. Make it."

Green took from his pocket the smartphone and sought in the memory of it the phone number to their person in San Francisco. He has done it quickly and waited over a minute, but no one answered. Here in New York were late hours, but in San francisco was the time three hours earlier. So, there was afternoon, and not sleeping time. It was strange why that man did not answer. This time Lambert paid attention to the attempt of Green. He has seen his effort and also was astonished. Why in fact that man is silent? Who can imagine, what is going over there?

"What will we do now?" Green stopped the calling and turned to Lambert waiting for answer.

"Yes. It is strange. I think we must stay here and waiting for the connection with him," said boss.

"Even whole night?" asked Green.

"We will wait and make a call every hour. That is all."

Lambert at the whole time was drinking slowly and after their conversation his glass became dry. So, he again approached to the table and second time poured the gin to it and stood a while looking ahead, without any move. It was irritable for Green. He expected from his boss more concrete action. Decision which could resolve current situation. But his boss was silent and did not talk. He seemed to be in another world. Again he swallow little amount of gin and then sat on the leather armchair. He felt tired himself. The age gave to know about itself. Lambert was not the young boy. His best days had gone like the wind. But consequently he was good boss. After many years of mutual work, they have been knowing each other like the same drop of water. Going neck to neck through the problems, they had together. And this time it seems to be the same. Green had best admirattion for Lambert. For his work and passion. Exactly saying their job wasn't legal. They were occupying with the spying techno-logical news, projects. In the industry. But aside, they have this one work, in the steel industry, but it was, as above-mentioned only the cover of their doing. It was nasty, bad work and they together were sticking in it for edges. But for many years they had the experience and weren't discovered by the government offfices. Everything was hidden. They operated in this field as a masters. It was their proper occupation. Again Lambert was looking ahead, and at last said.

"Try again. I need concrete situation. He must answer. By the way, did you pay for them sufficiently?"

"I did what you told," answered Green.

"So, we must wait," were next words of Lambert. He began to worry about this event. Green again took his smartphone and did as his boss ordered. He waited a moment, but this time was the same. Nobody answered.

"What do we now?"

His boss became more nervous, and the alcohol was making the effect, also.

"Yes. You had right. The matter is serious, We need to stay here whole night. Waiting for the connection."

"Do you think, someone has discovered our work?"

"I'm worried about this fact, and suppose, that it is truth." It was Lambert suggestion. At last he said it with misgiving. Keeping the glass in his palm, got up and began to walk in the study. Trying to think positively. He had, in the past many problems, but resolved it and making their job without any bad consequence. They acted in secret, and that was their proper income. But this time could be differently. Lambert thought deeply, and seems to be absent. There, in New York, now were late hours. And from the study of this skyscraper, were visible the lights of the city. It was beautiful to look on them. They made incredible feeling. Yes it was amusing, and no everyone had such splendid ocassion to relish with this view. So, they waited. Hour after hour the time was passing. And for Green it was getting more and more boring.

"Do you want one?" in certain moment his boss offered him glass of gin.

"No, sir," resigned Green. He was more worried about their situation. He tried to concentrate what to do next, and had not desire to drink. His boss did not pressure him. In the room was heard only the hum of air-condition, and they did not continue their conversation. The silence was making the atmosphere in it truly boring, and no one wanted to break it. Lambert again looked on the glass wall, behind which were seeing the light of the city. And in such way passed next hour.

"Try again," ordered for Green Lambert.

So, his subordinate took the smartphone in hand, and again made the same action, as before. He was waiting for a moment without any hope for success, keeping the phone at his ear, and when he wanted to break it, he heard, someone answered.

"Is that you? John Andrew?" Green almost was shouting to the telephone. Lambert, also, was moved, and became more vivid. At last they had connection with their man. The boss decided not to disturb in the conversation, because he wanted to be unknown for this man. He only looked on Green and with hope waited fo the explanations from this one. For his silence. At the same time Green was knowing more and more about the situation. He, after a moment became grey on the face, and Lambert has seen, there must be something wrong. The boss waited until the conversation will end… Green and their man were talking, yet. Slowly their dialogue was coming to the end. Green had known everything. Lambert was waiting for the results. Green rubbed his forehead and nervously began explain the whole situation. It wasn't nice. They had problem.

"The load did not come to the destination." Said Green.

"What has happened?" asked Lambert.

"He does not know exactly, but he had not met with the man from the port. So he has not clear evaluation of the situation."

Lambert stood for a while and suddenly turned to Green.

"You must go there." Unexpectedly he said. "Go to Teterboro and take the plane. Go to San Francisco and meet with him." Were the words of old man.

Green looked on his boss and thought, before him was the hard job. And how to resolve it? Now, when his boss decided about the journey he began to think how to prepare this one. He must to move the personnel of the plane. So he needed to go home and take the luggage. Now was late, then hours and he thought the crew and others will not be content about such decision. But it is necessity. And he called the pilots and stewards to be ready for the flight. Teterboro is the airport for the private aircraft. And they were keeping their jet plane "Embraer ERJ-175" in their private hangar. Green would have stayed in New York, but he needed to be obedient to the orders of his boss. He nodded and went out the same way, which they have arrived. He, also, had the same card, as a key, so, it was possible for him to do it. In his head were many different thoughts.

"What had happened over there?" he said to himself, when he was in elevator, trying to concentrate. First of all he needed to go home take the luggage and then ride to Teterboro. Maybe it will be nice to fly, and relish the splendid view through the window of the plane. Looking on the clouds and the blue sky. After several hours everything was ready. The crew was on their place preparing the jet plane and he, also, was in the hangar with his luggage. He waited for the last preparation to the flight. They took the fuel from cistern and reported their flight to the control tower. After certain time they had the permit for fly. Green was already inside of the plane, and fastened the seat belts. Yes, now he was ready to the flight. Before him was long journey with the between landing in Chicago on the O'Hare airport. For the refuelling. The Teterboro airport has two runway in the shape of letter X, so, they were driven by the control tower to one of them. After a moment they had the permission to takeoff. The plane quicker was increasing the speed and after a moment was in the air. Only the crew of their plane had said after several instructions to the control tower.

"Roger," in the nice voice.

CHAPTER 3

Kozinsky and Ford -it was the name of admiral, spent almost the whole twenty four hours, in hotel without any obstacles. They were in good humour and watching the tv, through the all time. And they waiting for the instruction from Washington. But it did not come, through their stay in hotel. The time went quickly and they even did not noticed how quickly. After their dinner in the room Ford and Kozinsky were talking about many events in their life. They had very interesting moments, and shared each other with pleasure with these facts. Kozinsky and Ford were in best mood and seemed such atmosphere wil not be didturbed by any bad things. They decided to stay in hotel room, because, they were waiting for the phonecall from the headquarters of FBI here in San Francisco. And of course the message from Washington. They fulled their time looking the television, and in that way they spent the waiting.

"Who could have predicted that it will repeat again?" thought admiral. "Maybe the same facts were in another places," he was thinking for example about the Europe, "who can predict?" was the same, and his next thought. It was like "Pandora Box". So, as disgusting as that thing. Trying only to stick into it the finger. Ford wanted now only to relax, and did not want to consider it. This is the matter of their President. He must take responsibility of this project. To resolve it. This was really confusion. Big confusion. And now they were waiting for farther events, what wiil happen next? And who is behind the whole case? It was difficult to foresee all aspect of their matter. At this moment nobody disturbed their repose. The telephone was silent. So they relished their nice time, and pressed the buttons of remote control of the tv set, taking the niceness of their sojourn in the "Nikko" hotel. They needed to stay right on the place, being accessible in any time, for the case, if someone will want to connect with them. Usually people play in the cards at such moment, but they hadn't this one. So, they spent their time only looking on the tv screen. In one moment, the admiral felt sick, but did not show it to commodore. He wanted to rest. After a while he recollected his former dream, in which he saw three sisters lying on the ground connected with their heads, and forming the letter T, with their bodies. At thee same time he felt incredible happiness, he did not experience that fact in his life. "Maybe it was nirvana?" went through his mind. "And what this is meaning?" was next thought. It was at night and lasted only several seconds. After that he woke very confused. And then was this strange phonecall from Kozinsky. He has been dressing quickly and waited for the arrival of helicopter. The commodore did not instruct him why he is sending the machine, but only said, it is very important case. It was conducive. The home of admiral was in California and near San Francisco, so, they hadn't many obstacles to do it. Making the flight possible. Admiral had his real estate over the long beach. It was convenient fact, the machine, could land on it. The whole process did not last long and after a half an hour they were over their purpose. Namely, the pier eighty. He now was in this hotel room waiting for the next events killing the time, looking the television. They together, Kozinsky and Ford were creating unanimous group, couple which could act positively at each trouble. They were content to work together. Of course Koziinsky was subordinate of admiral, and must to be obedient to this one. There were moments, he did not understand the orders of Ford, but at the end of many cases the admiral had the right, he had always the right decision and at the end the results were almost infallible. They were proper decision. And in such cases commodore saw the experience of admiral. So, they were together now, again. Neck to neck working each other. Ford was content, and for example the commodore had the same feeling. Involvement in their work and service in the navy. But after resolving the group of scientists engaged in the project "Golden Fleece" their ways separated and each of them went their own route. And above it admiral passsed on retire. So, they were on their own way of life. Sporadically keep contact each other. And now they were together in this hotel room talking and reminiscing the best moments of their common work. They had many facts to remember. Even joyful moments. They had many of them. So, in that way passed the time of their sojourn. In this hotel. It was nice to be together and talk each other of their job. Reminisce of the old days. And old facts of their service. For the commodore these were the moments to be nearer to the admiral person. To know him closer, and he had opportunity to come to a conclusion, his boss was a nice man, without any doubts. He knew him profoundly, now. There, they had their staying in this room, and speaking mutually about all things, even the future of next facts. They were trying to foresee what will happen to them and the whole process in which they were taking part... Many unknow facts. This was the uncertain time. They have been considering it without any doubts, it will be hard work, before them, and it was only one element, which made them sad. So, they had this one problem and trying to be prepared to it. The hours went quickly, and they did not even notice behind the window became more and more darrkly. They had a plan. The one of agents must call to them, if they had the message from Washington. So they waited and only waited for such message. Maybe it was irksome and not nice, but this one thing left for them. Yes, it was irksome. And they worried about it and again wait. Only wait.

CHAPTER 4

The Embraer ERJ-175 was flying over the clouds after the take-off from Chicago, from O'Hare airport, after the refueling. Martin Green took the glass of wine and was relishing the view behind the window of the aircraft. On the board of the machine were only him and the crew. He knew, the result of his journey depended from the meeting with their man from San Francisco. Green with him established their meeting at one of the garage of the SFO, the international airport of San Francisco., by phonecall. And now was flying to this town. He needed to concentrate on this one. He thought about it, and was not joyful of the consequence of this meeting. He rubbed his forehead and was trying to foresee, what he will know about the whole matter. It will not be good, He had thought. There, in the airport is so many possible place to meet, but they decided their meeting must not be monitoring by the cameras, and someone must to take him from this place. Maybe it will be short meeting, but he needed to do it not observing by others persons. He was in this airport several times already, so he know it best. And there, he knew how to find the way to the place of their meeting. Green was flying now considered all facts of this matter. Still looking through the window he has been drinking the wine and relished the nice view during their flight. He knew, they were flying over the many towns of United States and huge space of his country. Sporadically he saw the earth through the clouds, looking on it interesting what is under them. The hours were going quickly and he even did not notice when they wee ower the space of San Francisco. The pilots reducing the speed and called out the control tower of SFO. After a moment they had the permission to land. So, they again were reducing the ceiling of their flight. And began to approach to the twenty eight runway still going down gradually. From the control tower to the headphones of pilot came the words.

"Embraer I can presss you on the place of Delta they have the delay so go to terminal." After a moment the plane had landed, and theybegan to rolling to one of the terminals. Soon had the contact with the ramp one of them. Green unfasten the seat-belt, took his luggage and then went out the plane. He was already several times in this airport so had good orientation where to go farther. He was in domestic terminals, went through the check points and was in the main hall. He took the smartphone and called the man who was waiting for him. In the gates there were many people and could be felt the spirit of this airport. It was busy. And for someone, who could be for the first time in it, there, it could be confused find the way, for example how to get to the proper plane. SFO is big and great airport. International airport. Green quickly found himself on the adequate way to the garage And, by the elevator he get to the lower lever of this garage and pulled his luggage behind, began to seek the car of his man. He had not many troubles to find him. His man was on the proper place. After lleaving the elevator Green was joyful to find the way so quickly, and his man. He stood at his car waiting for him. Green shook the hand with him and was invited to inside of the auto. His man pointed the car, and after a moment they were inside. First of them said John Andrew—because it was the name of this man from San Francisco.

"I will tell you, what I know."

"I'm waiting," carefully answered Green.

"I was waiting for the man from port, during all the time." Again said Andrew. "And must disappoint you. The police intercepted our load. I know exactly, because this man from port saw some confusion around the ship. And no anyone could speak with these men from it. There, he has seen the soldier is staying at the ramp to the ship. So, you see, we have a problem."

"Do you think the FBI caught the load?"

"This is possible,"

Green rubbed his forehead and began to think of all the consequence of their situation. It was not nice.

"Do you have possibillity to penetrate to them?"

"I thought about such way,"

"And?"

"Dollar will do everything,"

Green thought quickly about whole affair, and came to the conclusion, they must act immediately.

"Try to know, if it would be possible. I need to know all about it. I said you, you would work quickly. In the past, and now we have a problem."

"I waited for my man whole night, and he related me the whole situation."

"May be in the bar," Green said it rudely

"I did all possible thing. If you would know, what had happened."

"It is the pupil in the eye for me, act quickly and with all strength. This is your obligation," this time Green was not nice and pressed Andrew more.

"That is all what you need?"

Green did not answer, and wanted to figure what to do next. What he will tell for Lambert? He worried about this. And after a moment decided to return to New York.

"Have you more sugggestion?" he asked.

"No. I understood everything," answered Andrew.

"So, go to work. And I must go back to my firm. You took so many money, and I need concrete results from you. Do it right now," it wasn't nice speech of Green. "We have a problem, and you must resolve it." After that he opened the door of car and got out without any explanation. Again he went the same way as before, but this time he wanted to go back to one of the domestic terminals at which will be possible to return to his aircraft. He had contact with pilot by the telephone. He stayed in one of terminals, until his plane will be attached to one of the ramps. So, his journey did not benefit and with such message he was returning to New York. He needed to wait half an hour, until he got the permission to went to the gate and on the board of his plane. Again one of the passenger planes of domestic airline had the delay and control tower gave for them the possibility to takeoff. Soon he was inside of his aircraft and was prepared to the start. Through the window he has seen, how the plane was disconnected from the ramp and then taxied on the way to the runway. On the Charlie taxiway. Soon they were on runway and started to fly. Second after second the plane rushed more and more and soon was in the air. The control tower gave them wishes of good flight and after a moment disconnected with the crew. Green unfastened the seat belt, and then spread his legs making more comfortable himself. He needed a rest. So, after a while lying on the bed inside the plane, he again began to think about whole matter. It was complicated.

"What will I say for Lambert?" he said to himself, "maybe I go back too quickly? And would to stay in San Francisco longer? But Lambert will want to have the relation soon, I'm sure." In such mood Green returned to New York worried about the reaction of his boss. He supposed this one will not be satisfied with the result of his journey. What will bring the nearer future? He had many question unanswered. Trying to calm himself and prepare such relating as simple as it was possible. Being at a loss to resolve these questions he was in bad humour. Now he tried to retrieve the best state of his mind, but it wasn't easy. They needed to suspend their activity and through the whole flight he was thinking about this matter. HIs and Lambert's problem. He had it now in his mind. They, after a several hours flew over Chicago airport waiting for the permission to land and refueling. And soon got it. So, after a certain time again they were in the air and towards New York. Martin Green was waiting all the time, during such operation, and staying aboard, inside the plane. Truly explaining, he was not interesting in the whole process, there, on the land, and he knew everything is in the hands of his crew. And now they were flying towards New York at the night. He heard only the hum from engines and saw the light of moon. Maybe this time it was nice, and he had the opportunity to relish of such view, now, and for the moment did not think about problems. It was splendid, amazing and very impressive view through the windows of his jet plane. So, he had a better mood, not disturbed by anything. But the thought about last event, with Andrew, the meeting with him again moved him profoundly. He had no peace even now, and he, needless to say, had anxiety what to say for Lambert. He began to collect the thoughts and preparing in his mind to foresee, how Lambert will act. It was, the matter in the hands of his boss. And Green had the feeling it will not be nice. What about the consequence in the nearer future? If FBI had their load, they will be searching, who is behind whole project. And they will not stop to investigate, to know about everything concerning the matter. Now everything was posible. He felt something stuck in his stomach. It was not nice. He felt worse than before. It was, also, his problem. So, he saw, they must stay together to be prepared for any worst thing. He thought:

"What to do now?" his next thought was, "I need to picture whole matter as not impotant as it is possible, for Lambert. He will be angry, so, I must to pacify him for the first moment. Of course he will be wanting to know all about it, and I need to be prepared for his humour," Green was tired and his head did not work quickly. He was not drunk, even if he took the alcohol to much. Through the last minutes he thought all about the meeting with Lambert and tried to be sober. He foreseen his boss maybe will be angry and he worried about such fact, but again tried not disturb the nice moment of his journey. Now he was inside of the jet plane and looking on the moon and whole view behind the window. The light of moon and the clouds made impressive picture for his eyes, so, he decided not to think and worry about the last meeting. Only relish of the scenery before him. Yes, it was nice, and proper for his state of mind. Continuing the flight they were nearer the end of their journey. New York was approaching to them with every minute. So, they were more peaceful it was spent without any accident. The plane was in best state, and no one was concerned about any surprise. They were flying over the territory of United States high about several kilometres above the earth. The flight was, as above-mentioned, without any obstacles, and was boring. During the whole time. They approached to the destination minute after minute. To the Teterboro. It was enough for them. And they wanted to finish the flight. The journey was going to end, and they were tired caused by whole work of the day. Actually it was busy day. And above all, the crew had not the opportunity to relax, because Green was acting so quickly, so, they work already over twenty four hours. They needed the rest, but, they must listen to him, and act according with his orders. It was not easy to work under such pressure, but first of all they must to fulfil what he has been saying to them. So, they now again were at the helm of their aircraft, and approached to Teterboro. On the face of one of the pilots, appeared the smile, when he has thought about the end of their flight. Soon they were intercepted by the control tower of Teterboro and their flight was controled by it. The control tower led them this time, ordered to minimize the speed of flight and reduce the ceiling, when they were nearer the runway. It was lit and the whole operation of landing was not difficult for them. They needed to fly according to the instructions of control tower, second after second they approached to the main-one of the two, runways. And after a moment, after a landing they were on the earth everybody lucky, the journey came to the end. They now only needed to roll to the hangars, and to stay there, until Green after taking the luggage went out of this aircraft. For him was waiting the limousine also near the hangar, so, he was happy from such fact, he will not be waiting for the car, and quickly sat inside the auto with little smile on his face. Yes, it was pleasure again to be on the ground after safe trip, in the air, and relish go home, take even a shower and later go to the sleep. Green knew, he will meet with Lambert early in the morning, so, he had several hours of repose in his own house. When he was already in the limousine, he concentrated on the last events. Considering all, what were in his mind, he came to the conclusion, it will be difficult to relate whole situation for Lambert, not cause the anger of his boss. Green knew, Lanbert had the inclination to fall into bad mood, disturb good aatmosphere in the bureau, and he urgeed all his staff to work. He also knew, he must be prepared for the meeting with fresh conclusion and evaluation of the situation. So, he needed to repose and take, even several hours of sleep. He was trying to think positively about his future meeting. Maybe Lambert will not be angry. Through the whole time, when the limousine was approaching to his home, he was in such mood considering it. And in that way he arrive to his house. Being inside, he did everything what he planned before, taking shower after undressed and went to the bed. In the first moment he could not fall in the sleep, but later it came itself. For him left only to dream in peaceful way not disturbed by anything, carried him to the another unnatural world. Yes, it was nice. Very nice, and slowly the night went through and the morning came to him and his reality. Preparing him for the future next day.

CHAPTER 5

For Kozinsky, there was, nothing to do. He went to his own room, leaving the admiral. The hours passed quickly and immediately became the evening. Outside was dark. And he did not notice that was eight o'clock. He was alone and did not want to sleep. He sat on the bed and thought. Their situation is not so bad, but what will bring the future? In reality the facts concerning the matter were not worse, than someone could predict. Kozinsky now realized after several hours, when he has seen the programm on the tv, there was, some way, to exit from such bad situation. Everything will be in the government hands.

"So, don't worry," he thought. He looked on the affair more profoundly, than before. Of course, he was aware of the danger. Of this matter, but not so much, as could be seen. Trying to relax he thought about going to the lobby, maybe for some drink. Truly saying, now he had feeling to do it. It was his desire. In spite of late hour, he had done it. So, concentrated on it, he decided to make it. He took the magnetic card and went out the room, and has gone to the elevators position. Time was going quickly, and after a moment he was in the lobby. There was any person, only from the depth flew the romantic sound of Beatles "Yesterday" played on the piano. He stood at the reception desk and looked around, and after a moment he saw, there in the center of lobby, where were placed the armchairs, has been sitting one person. It was woman. But she was sitting back to him, so he did not see her face.

"Maybe she is beautiful," he thought, and was trying to learn about it. Nothing came to his mind, how to know her, but after several socond he had idea what to do to find out it. He looked around, and ascertained there was any person in the lobby, only he and this woman. He simply shuffled with his leg and deliberately made it loud having hope, this woman will react on it. And when he had done it this woman really acted according to his anticipation. She turned the head being curious what has happened behind her. At this moment Kozinsky saw her face. And his prediction became truth. He immediately was seeing the beauty. He did not disappoint himself of this view. So, for him stayed only to approach to her and begin the conversation. Truly, it was difficult moment for him to invent something how to start such speaking, but he decided to go farther and to make the acquaintance with this woman. He came to her and said:

"Excuse me, may I join?" for a while there was some kind of uncertainty. This woman looked on him a little curious waiting a moment to answer but later she decided to invite him with the nod showing she was intelligent woman and kind. Even if she hadn't the desire to talk with him, she did not show it still curious what this man could expect from her. Kozinsky felt better after this invitation and had courage to go farther in his doing. He looked for the words what say next feeling a little anxiety how this woman will react for his speech.

"I'm looking for the information about San Francisco," there, he needed to start the conversation somehow, so, he invented this kind, the way, to do it. Maybe it is strange, he did it in such way. And it was obvious for her this man needed to pick up this woman.

"Sure, you can sit down," there was, her answer.

"You know, I can get the information from guidebook, but I'm looking for the place more curious and not conventional, so I thought, when I saw you…maybe you are the person who know the town, and could help to realize my plans."

She looked on him showing a little surprise for such words and with a hesitation answered:

"Sorrry, but I'm not adequate person, what you looking for." And with a smile added, "I must disappoint you." She was gentle and moreover very beautiful, black hair and wearing long, in light colour robe. Her hands were delicate, but she had a little nervous movements, and it was showing she was in the state of little uncertainty. Kozinsky looked on her fingers, and he saw she had no the ring. So this fact encourage him to go farther in his intention. He sat on the opposite leather armchair and still continued the conversation. He was single and this woman, for sure, was the same. So this facts made easier for him to make a friendship with her. He was tense and a little uncartain about the results of this meeting. But first ices were broken.

"I thought, when I saw you…you are from this town," he still continued in the same way the conversation. Sure it was all only pretext. He did not want to cut their talk, and keep it having hope it will be positive to achieve his purpose. This woman was looking like the First Lady of United States. It was his impression. And again he said in delicate way.

"Excuse me, madam…" in this moment he hesitated for a while. He thought he can be boring man for her, so quickly, was seeking proper words in his mind, to be interested for her. "I am the man who does not know precisely this town. And I was thinking, you can be person who can help for me." He obviously lied, but for him she was so intrigued minute after minute, and he had feeling like a boy, who is in front of a teacher doing exam.

"Sorry, I am from another town. II have business in San Francisco, and I…" at this moment she broke her speak, also, hesitating to say more, and for the first time she looked on Kozinsky face to face made impression she does not know what this man wants from her. Commodore quickly noticed such fact and trying not to break the conversation he answered:

"Excuse me, I did not introduced myself. My name is Alfred Kozinsky. I am commodore and work in the navy. It is rude I did not make it before." He ended to speak watching her reaction. Yes, she was impressed, but trying to hide it. By the way, she did not know what to do. To keep the acquaintance or not. So, she moved on the armchair a little nervous showing, she was uncertain. After that she said her name, also, for him, but he heard only, the first name, gave him her hand and welcomed him. And that was enough. Little smile appeared on the face of commodore He felt himself encouraged. But from her side could be seen, she was not interested to continue such conversation. Kozinsky has not been resigning even seeing it. For him it was occasion to meet such beautiful woman. And he tried to use whole his art to keep this meeting. Several minutes passed, and he was now speaking about not so much important things. Only having the hope, he did not waste the time. It was hard for him to predict the reaction of this newly picked up girl. On her face appeared the smile and then desappeared. He again was not certain what to do. He rather was not belonging to the men who give up after first failure. So., he decided again to go farther in this way of courtship. Trying to be nice, not rude. Did not think about failure. And above all he was chatmed of her beauty. But after several minutes he felt, she was not interested to continue this conversation and was boring. That was the fact, he did not know what to say farther. He saw, her face became, could be said, long and impressed, her hesitancy, concerning his person.

"Again bad shot?" he thought. And really it was true. For him left only to cut this talk and go out from the place. Obviously she was not curious to continue this conversation. She only agreed what he said and did not encourage him, showing her disapproval. Of course she was not interested to keep this acquaintance farther and was a little nervous after several minutes of this talking. Kozinsky noticed that fact and did not know wat to say more. He tried simply pick up her, and was looking for the way not break the meeting. But for him it was not easy to fulfil such adventure. Yes, she was nervous, and she showed it. And than it was obvious, he must resign to do next courtship. He looked on her with desapproval and then thanked her for these several, nice minutes. He stood and not giving for her his hand, only expressing his respect, left her thanking for such meeting. At this moment he felt tiredness, and again thought about sleeping. So, not longer concerning this fact, he made a decision to go to his room dissatisfied of the last time, namely meeting with this girl, and going slowly to the elevators, was trying not to worry about it. When he was in the cabin, this last episode did not make on him any impression. He had, even now good mood, and tried to think about their job. Yes, it was nice to meet such beautiful woman, and he only smiled on last fact. It would be nice to keep acquaintance with such beauty, but not everything in the life was possible. So, he was not very disappointed what had happened. Not every battle can be won. During his consideration, after a while the door had opened, and he went out of the cabin. And was on the same corridor as before. When he was going down to the lobby. After a while he stood at the door of his room. He opened it and went inside. Now was late hours of the night. So, he began undress, still thinking about this woman.

"She was cold as iceberg," went through his mind. "Maybe she is waiting for the prince from fable," was his last thought, when he was in bed, and then fell in sleep.

CHAPTER 6

Robert Lambert woke at the seven o'clock. He had rather nice sleeping, so, he was ready to work immediately and was in good mood… He had certain dream but he did not remember it. As usual it was not important. He dressed and went to the eating room to take the breakfast. It lasting half an hour, and he did not hurry at it. When he finished it, he took the newspaper and looked on the page, where was printed the quotation of the Wall Street. Fom the former day. As usual the each index was down. Nothing interesting on the stock exchange. And than he only looked on the page with financial news, briefly. He saw every index was going down. At this moment he felt some kind of anxiety. Only troubles. Over there, on the Wall Street as usual, was nothing so interesting. To the open of stock exchange he had one hour. It will be opened at nine o'clock as always. So he was doing the same things through several years. He went out of his house, and approached to the limousine. Which stood at the gate of his real estate. He did not hurry, knowing he has much time to be at his office. And of course he did not know, Green was after his journey and waiting for him. The people could think, he was hard-working man, but it is false fact concerning his doing. In the late years of his work he was not so quick to make decision, as was in the former days. He had built his empire all the time, and now had the concern. Was he doing the right things? Or maybe all was big mistake. That was his consideration. And when he sat in the car, this thought accompanied him. Yes, he had problem. Will the project "Golden Fleece" resolve it? He had hope, it will. It was like magnet magnetizes the iron. And it attracted him with such strength. For the while he was sitting without any move, when the car was riding toward his tower block.

"Maybe I get the information from Green?" came through his mind. And for relax he turned on his personal computer, which was fastened inside of his limousine. At this time, it was after nine o'clock, he made a connection with his dealer at the stock exchange, and wanted to see latest news from it. He got it quickly and began the conversattion with his man at the Wall Street.

"Nothing interesting, "he heard from computer. It was the voice of his dealer. And really, on the screen were showed the latest quotations, not so interesting as he wished for himself. So, he looked on them quickly, and then turned down the computer. Meanwhile the car was approaching to his skyscraper. They were near it and when the driver covered the distance between his house and the building, he again thought about the journey of Green.

"What is he doing now?" he asked himself wasn't aware, Green was in New York at this time. After a moment they were at the building, and the car stopped on the parking, at the place correctly made for them. The driver got out of the car and then opened the door of limousine for his boss making easier for him to get out of the auto. Lambert got off the car and went to the entrance of the building. Before it stood many others cars belonging to the workers of his firm. He approached to the door, from the glass and after a moment was inside. And again as before went through the post of guard going to the elevators. When he was at the place where were these ones he chose this one special belonging only to him, and after a while was on the proper storey with this magnetic key in his hand, and with its help found on the proper level. The door has been opening, and he could step it the same corridor as always. No one informed him about arrival of Green. And no one was aware of his arrival. So, he went next to his study not giving information for his secretary about his coming. He wanted to have a half an hour of quiet, silent time of staying here in his study. Not disturb by anyone. He needed it utterly. So, he sat in his armchair considering the last events.

"Maybe are some news from Green?" he thought. And after this half an hour, he decided to call to his secretary. To know it, he connected with this one. And really, after a while the secretary, this was a woman informed him about the arrive of Green. He was astonish of the fact, his subordinate was again, after such short journey, here in the office. He quickly ordered for her to summon Green to him and having good thoughts was waiting for him, did not even drink his usual gin. He expected good news. Not bad. He had hope it is productive-the flight of his subordinate. And he was, at this moment in better mood. He does not expect wrong message. But, how he was in wrong conviction, he did not even foresee. Yes, this trip had bad results. And he did not know it. After a several minutes Green stood before him.

"I haven't good news, sir," were the first words of his subordinate.

Lambert looked on him with strange feeling, did not believe what he heard. He was astonished. From the words of Green he came to a conclusion, their problem was really serious. He had now conviction, they must to withdraw from this project "Golden Fleece".

"How did that happen?" was his thought. "So much work, and it wil go in fiasco now?" He was really worried about this fact. "What do you suggest?" he asked Green.

"I repeat again. We must obliterate every trail concerning this matter. And resign from this project. FBI will be looking for us. Who is behind this one. They will be looking for, who is sponsoring that affair, and I think they will not rest until they will find us. That is all," answered Green. And later added, "it was good idea, we divided the contact with co-workers of this matter. Maybe they will not give information about us. I am sure they don't know of this fully. Only the shreds."

"Yes you have the right." In low voice said Lambert, "I understand everything. We have a problem." He added.

Now, at last to the mind of Lambert came conscious of the situation in which they were.

"We must be prepared to everything in the future," Green has said, "so we need to concentrate on the next plan To cut every connecion with those people. Over there in San Francisco. It is possible they will be know even about our plant on Bali everything was prepared with such details, and I don't know why did that happen."

The day began very sadly for them, and they were conscious, everything was in ruin. There, in the future were not view for bettersituation. Lambert this time again took the glass of gin trying to pacify himself. For him it was like strike with heavy hammer. His all hope with this project was waste. So much time and money were lost. Without any success. And they were so near. Now, they needed to save their own situation. The FBI will be looking for them, it was sure, and they must to concentrate all effort on the possible way of defence.

"Who could predict it will not success?" thought Lambert. He looked on the Green and felt discomfort. His nice and easy life can be disturb by this project. He knew it and was conscious how important this matter was for him in the current and future time. He needed be careful and will not do false action. Wait and don't do any move? Maybe it will be better to act in that way. He tried to calm down and don't worry about it in such high anxiety. What will be in the next time? Who know? Such situation was not, for sure, conducive for his state of health. At this time he felt tiredness. So, sat in the leather armchair, still keeping the glass of gin in his hand and drank slowly. Trying to find the way to exit from this inconvenient situation. In his hidden job they had many trick and ways, if they will be in the possible troubles. To exit. Green looked on Lambert hoping this one will invent some way to resolve this problem. Yes, he had a hope. The time passed quickly and they were thinking now about this last event. But no one of them had any idea how to exit from that bad situation. Lambert knew, he must throw away the dreams of using the machine "Golden Fleece" for his own purposes. Now he had some kind of perplexity. Why this project is dangerous for the world? He had no any idea. They, he and Green invented together to use their means and have benefit from that occasion. They did not foresee, there, in the future will be any problem with it. So, they wanted to do it. Continue. They found Patrick Silva and were knowing about his financial problem. They accted in such way. At the beginning of their work everything was going good. They eliminated any possible obstacles. So, they excluded such farther failure. And now they had this problem. Everything made before was wrong. And that was their result. The time passed quickly and they even did not notice, it was midday. Green looked on his boss waiting for any decision from him. But this one was sitting behind his desk dully staring ahead. And showing, he had not any idea how to go out of their bad position.

"We do need only wait until police will appear at our door." He concluded. They both were in the same mood and trying to foresee what will be in the near future. They had no idea what to do now. It would be better, to be in the next days, to stay away of their activity in the whole affair. Lambert after this suffering time stood up and still with the glass in the hand began walking. He needed the time to consider everything. Maybe the police will not discover their truth? Who is behind the whole business? Yes, he had only the emptiness in his mind.

"Who could have predicted that it will happen?" he asked himself in silence. There were many thoughts in his head not important at this time. He began to walk to and fro. All the time trying to invent the way to exit from this difficult situation. However he was after good night, at this moment he was feeling tired. It was difficult to describe the state of his mind. There was the time of anxiety, they together were occupying only with this one thought, how to get out of this bad situation. Needed only to find the way to resolve it positively. For them left only to take a good lawyer, and be prepared for any event in such case. Lambert again took next glass of gin and looked on Green. This one was sitting calmly on leather armchair without any move. And he looked like last disaster. His black suit was in disarray. And he kept position, as if would swallow the stick, needed to concentrate on better thing. And he had hope, his boss will find the way to go out of their troubles. So, Lambert seeing it, also felt the same state of spirit. Truly saying, they had what they wanted. They would to count with the consequences of their doing. To foresee what will happen in the future. And have the concept how to resolve if it would have appeared. It was difficult time for them. And now they had the results. It was like the ride on the motocross. Very quickly and dangerously. They would be prepared for such occasion. It was not nice at this moment. The time went quickly and did not work for their benefit. They were walking like in the labyrinth. In the addition not lighted. Their emotions were mixed. And withut any concept. Without any exit.

"Where you met Andrew?" asked Lambert.

"In the garage A," answered Green and added, "don't worry. There were not any cameras," with little tremble in his voice he said.

"So, in the future, there will not be any evidence, you have met him."

"I hope so,"

"I think, there will not be the reason to worry about your travel to San Francisco. What you think?" asked Lambert.

"I think you have not any reason to worry about such fact."

"I have only the cause to worry about Silva and the others. What will they say for police? They will say everything about the plant in Indonesia."

"I think we must inform them about this all fact and evacuate the personel. And we must do it quickly."

"You have right."

"So, I must go to our service room and connect with them. We need to hide any trail concerning us." Slowly Green suggested.

"You think about liquidation of all?"

"We have worst scenario, which we planned.," after a while Green said., "so I suggest to do it."

"Did you think about this all disorder?"

"Have you a better idea?"

Lambert at last sat behind the desk without any question. It was worst moment in his life. He had so much hope with the project "Golden Fleece". But now everything laid out in ruin. He counted so much on it. And now he would resign from it. Who could predict it? He was staying face to face with defeat. Surely it was worst event in his life. And he spent so much money for that. The whole project gave him so much energy, hope and better views on the future. He was dreaming about it like little boy. Making perspectives, plans how to use it and have profit from it. And now he must to say good by to these dreams. He was sad and only had one thought. To rest. Yes, it was difficult moment for him. And now someone must clean up everything what he has done. They all-he and Green were so much close to the end of victory. Each of them had the same feeling. To win. But now, it was obvious they were defeated. And what to do now? To take all the consequences of their work. They were now occupied with the thoughts what to do next. They were planning to connect with Bali.

"Go to service room and inform them about liquidation plan. We need to make it. Everything is going wrong."

"I will go. Maybe it is not neccessary, but we need to make it, okay?"

And than, when he has said it he went out of the study of his boss, and later went to the same elevator as before, to make the order of Lambert. After a several minutes he was on the storey on which was the service room. He went to it and without any invitation with the personnel approached to the chief of their workers, of the room, and ordered for him to send the message, which they decided with Lambert. For the first moment the chief was astonished what he heard, but he was the subordinate of Green and without any question ordered for one of their workers to fulfil the order. They had some kind of cipher, so, he needed to wait several minutes to code it and send the message. The order was strange for him, but he did what was demanded from him. Without any question. The code was simple and it took several minutes to do it. So, the message was made and sent. Green for the first moment felt some kind of relief. He was satisfied. Maybe they will hide their action before the police will discover their job. The decision was difficult for them, but they needed to make it It was obvious. Green felt through his skin the next troubles. And it was right decision. To liquidate the plant and their workers. To hide any trail of their activity. Lambert and Green were prepared for such event. They planned it if it will happen. So, it was right decision, they could make. And now left for them only to wait what will be, in the future. The project "Golden Fleece" for them was over. Green only could imagine what kind of troubles will be in fact. Worst scenario began. And he concluded and had hope the police will not find any trail of his and Lambert connection with this matter. But it was only small hope. He knew, Silva and the others will say everything for police. He was sure. About that fact. Many month of preparing this project, and money went in thin air. They had only ruin. For him stayed to seek proper way how to hide himself. Even to leave Lambert with his own troubles, the firm and wait until everything will end. Yes, it was not honest, and he felt himself like a rat running from sinking boat, but what he can do? In the face of such fact. He needs to rescue. Without any help. He had in his nose the interest of Lambert and the firm. If police will discover their activity and connection with this whole matter, no one will help him. Even Lambert. So, for him left only to think about his own skin. Of course, he had some options in the case when he will be in troubles. But now everything was possible. And maybe the firm will cope with this problem even this time. So he has not certainty what to do. And after giving the order for his staff he decided to think it over in the latter time. Truly it was not nice period. For him and Lambert and the concern. He went back to the elevator and after several minutes was again in the boss study. He informed him about last action and was seeing the sadness of this old man. Green wanted to make everything what is possible to comfort him, but anything came to his mind to do it. Now, he again had no any idea to improve the situation, and the atmosphere in the study was gloomy. The time was going quickly and they did not notice the day passed hour after hour approaching to the twelve o'clock. Lambert was a little tipsy. Green noticed it and it was not proper for his mood. But he did not make any remark for his boss, only ignored that fact.

"I sent the message," he informed him with low voice.

"Okay. We will wait for the answer. It will take some time. So, I think…" at this moment he stopped for a while, with blunt look ahead and keeping the glass in his hand, he added, "they will inform us about the situation. I think they will be observing what will take place. We can't break the connection with them. I want to know about everything. What do you suggest?"

"I have the same idea," answered Green.

"So, you see, we must act in such way, don't permit the police to know about us."

"I agree with you," Green felt better for this moment. They together this time were feeling some kind of relief and mutually thought in the same way. Maybe that was best to resolve it positively. It was good idea, they did not take part personally in the contact with the rent people and don't have the reason to worry about such fact. For Green, in person it was enough for one day. And moreover he was after trip. He needed to rest and don't worry about this case. Better to leave this matter for Lambert. It was his idea to begin the project. So, he must to worry about the future of whole matter. And they will not stay in the bureau the whole day. No one demanded it from them. Greeen counted for Lambert. He looked on his wristwatch and saw. It was one o'clock pm.

"I need to go home," he said.

"Yes, sure. You made enough for me…" Lambert with little hesitation answered.

So, Green understood these words as a permission to go out. Without shaking hands he went out of the study of Lambert. And after a moment he was in his own room. Took the raincoat and was ready to go out from the building. On the parking, before the skyscraper stood his own sedan He sat inside it and nervously grasped his hands on the steering-wheel. And felt comfort. This time without any supervision over him. He had plan, first to go home, and then, maybe over there to drink a beer. He had a desire to do it. And after half an hour was in his second home-apartment near the central park. He thought it could be the last occasion to do it. But he did not worry of his situation. Was it bad? Maybe. In fact there was some reason to feel gloomy, but he was tough and it not made on him any impression, concerning the last troubles, in his firm. He needed only to rest and had as above-mentioned to drink such beer. Yes this time it was nice, to feel comfort and not think about whole day as a wasted hours. Minute after minute was better. The alcohol made him joyful after arrive to the apartment. He lay on the bed and began smile. Maybe the police will not find their involvement in this matter. He became cheerful. And after that fell asleep.

CHAPTER 7

In San Francisco were the small hours. But admiral and Kozinsky were awake and after the breakfast. They were waiting for the message from the headquarters of FBI. They wanted to wait and not move from the hotel. After good slept night the admiral was feeling fresh and relaxed. But Kozinsky only felt the consequences of the night meeting with this one not knowing woman. he, also in spite of this fact was ready to the new day. They wanted to stay in their rooms, so long, as they could. The time of sojourn was nice nd they felt comfort and pleasure of such fact. After breakfasst, they again were looking the television and tried to concentrate, to predict what will be next, in the near future. They both were absorbing about it, the whole matter and what will come in the next hours. It was difficult to foresee that fact. Maybe they will get the answer for that thing by telephone or one of the agents, directly here in their hotel room. Someone from the agents will arrive to them and will inform our men what is going on? They expected to get onformation from FBI right here, so, they don't want to go out from the hotel. Only wait for the message. They must be present in this moment, here in the room. Without any surprise. And that was the reason why they were staying here in hotel occupying only with watching the television screen. But this time in it there, was not some interesting programms so, they felt how boring was the time. Though the working hours just began, to them no one was calling. They were waiting only. Ready for the meeting with Snowden or other agent. They expected only about that fact. And absorbing with such thing. The hours were going slowly, even they killed the time with watching the television, but to them wasn't going anything. Any break in that state. So, it was really boring time. They concluded, the three agents, sent to this matter, must be occupying with something, and that is why they don't connect with admiral and commodore. Or maybe they neglect the fact, about this matter, to arrive to them. To the hotel.

"I need to drink something," at one moment said Kozinsky.

"I will ask about it the reception," told the admiral. Offered his help in request of Kozinsky.

"If you wish," was the thank of the last.

So, admiral took the receiver and pressed the button connecting with reception. After a while of speaking he put it on the table ending the speech. He ordered what Kozinsky was asking. He felt the same. The desire to drink something. Maybe cola? Why not? Now they can afford it. The firm will pay. And after some moment, to their door knocked the waiter. Also with the glasses. It was full comfort. He placed the cola and glasses on the table and turned to the exit. Admiral gave him ten dollars of a tip and again they were lonely. Mutually they drank it slowly relishing with the taste of it, and continuously waiting for their man from the headquarters of FBI here in San Francisco. They had desire to meet with them as quickly as possible. No one can forget that this present matter needed to be resolved like the speed of light, eloquently said. And no one can foresee what will be the results of such game. They both, Ford and Kozinsky took part in it and were on the first line of that affair… They knew most about it and were necessary, in person to be in this interrogation of Silva and others, present, at it. So, they predicted they will be participants in farther etap of this case. Again, they were looking on television and considering all facts of the matter in which they now were participating. Admiral foresaw the next days of their action, and knew, it will be their duty to work at that affair. He nd Kozinsky were fully convinced, it will be necessary from the government side to consider such fact. It is their oblligation to be present, in the future, at this matter They were experienced at that work. It is obvious, they took part in it in the past. So, in their minds were the thoughts, they must be prepared to the next days. Of co-operation. And everything in the life, so far, must be thrown away. Admiral and of course Kozinsky had many their own plans, what to do, but right now, this matter made them to give all their strength to this case. And give up from their own, personal plans. They needed to concentrate on the current time and events. It was obvious. And on the future. But it was hard to predict any possible ways, how the matter will be continued in next days. So, they foreseeing, it will bring many unexpected facts. And they must be prepared for that.

"What do you think?" in certain moment asked Kozinsky.

"Nothing so much impotant," answered Ford, a little confused about this question, and added, "I think only of our sojourn, here in the hotel. Isn't funny?"

"Yes, I think the same. But I'm a little nervous. The time is going and our friends don't arrive. The waiting for them is so difficult, and I am impatient from that reason. What are they doing? they forget about us?"

"Don't worry. Everything will be all right." Said Ford, but he, also, was nervous.

These words did not make Kozinsky calm. The waiting was so bad for his mood and even he was a little angry to waist the time. Only waiting and waiting. The television did not interest and not absorbed his atttention. He wanted too be present at the farther proceeding over there in the headquarters of FBI. He was a active man and such state, at this moment was for him difficult. He wanted to be there right now, immediately. For example to know more from Silva about whole affair. Maybe he did not say everything and were some elements moreover it. He took the remote control and turned down the television. And at this moment became quiet atmosphere. They could talk without such noise. They needed gather their thoughts and think in more pleasand way. At once the mood in the room became nice. Ford smiled for such act seeing, his commodore was angry. So, what to do now? Showing anxiety? And with pleasurable voice he was trying to pacify his suboordinate.

"Don't worry. Everything will be all right."

"Why they don't give any signal for us? I think, it is not so right from their side," answered commodore slowly sitting in an armchair. For him obviously was it so much inconvenient to stay in such atmosphere. And when they were considering this fact, to the door some-one knocked. At once they pay attention to that, and commodore approached to the door and opened it. He has seen in entrance one of the agents. It was Snowden. Commodore looked on him a little astonished, surprised.

"Good morning gentlemen," it were first words of Snowden. After that commodore withdrew and let him go into the room. Also, the admiral was surprised seeing him at that hour.

"Good morning," they both answered. "We are waiting for you Mr. Snowden," added Ford. And then they all shook hands, wel-comed him to inside.

"I have some information for you. And I know you waited for me...," hesitantly began the conversation Snowden. "To us arrived the men from Washington. And I wanted to tell you about it, and to take you to headquarters."

"It is splendid message. We were waiting for that." This was the voice of admiral. He and Kozinsky began to pick up their personal things, by the way, they had not many of them, and after a several minutes they were ready to go with Snowden. Admiral was a little curious what a men are they? These men from Washington. At that thime, he did not ask Snowden about this fact, engaged the way, they were going. It took several minutes when they were in the car after settle the affairs at the reception. And now they were going to the headquarters of FBI. Ford knew, he will know all about such men on the place. The day was nice and they were for the first time outside, because they spent all the time in the hotel room. So, Snowden was driving the car and they needed to pass several crossroads to be in the destination. The building of FBI was not so far from the hotel, and the riding lasted a short time to be there. During this riding admiral was thinking about the meeting with the men from Washington. Snowden was silent occupying with the driving, and he was paying attention to it. On his face were only the signs of tiredness. Through the last several days he had worked hardly sacrificing his precious time to these recent events. Considering all things only he was mak-ing good job. The others two agents appointed to this affair were not so eager to work in the way as he was doing. It had, also, a good sides. He has now some kind of pleasure to be at this affair and did not occupy with the boring, dull job, which he so far was doing. Yes, it was positive some sort of change and even interesting, but until now he did not understand why it is so important. He only understood, he must give all his strength to that. So, he was making it with a sacrifice, not pretend and wanted to help for the admiral and commodore. And during these considerations the time has gone and they had found utterly on the place. He stopped the auto at left side of the avenue, stalled the car engine and next they sat out of the car. Went to the entrance of the building still not talking only wanted to be in the correct room in which they could meet with the men from Washington. After a while they were on the place. Admiral was a little surprised, when he learned, who they were. But did not show his astonishment. They were the officers of United States Air Force Office of Special Investigation. Shortly "OSI". They shook hands and went to the farther details of this matter.

"We must take your prisoners to the "Andrews Base", we have such order," said one of the officers.

Admiral did not show his next astonishment. Why to the "Andrews", was his thought? But did not show his surprise.

"We have transport. Correctly saying the plane. And we will take your load to that base. You must be informed, the President wants to talk with you, Mr. admiral." One of officers of OSI said to Ford. "Also, your companion must go with us," he added.

Admiral was happy, the matter is going so quickly, and he was content, the President knows already about their problem. The matter obviously was so important, and the head of state must be informed about whole event. After a sojourn in the hotel Ford was relaxed and ready to the co-operation. It was good message. Everything is going after his thought. So, only left for them to download the pack to the plane and fly to Washington. He and Kozinsky, now wanted to be at the whole process. To be present at this all event. And they were content fully, these men from "OSI", needed to take them. The investigation must be confidential and kept in secret. Now, they had the beginning of whole story, and what will bring the future was big enigma. So, they; admiral and commodore felt it was good, they will be in the farther process. Admiral, now began to think about the meeting with President. How it can be prepared, he did not know. Maybe for the first time he will be in the Oval Office? Who could have predicted that it will happen? It was very important moment in his and Kozinsky life. Correctly saying they were in the center of this history. And can be proud from this fact. And had big responsibility in playing such role. So, in spite of many difficulties they wanted to resolve the problem with "Golden Fleece" project.

"We have a Hercules C-131 and the machine is now at SFO airport. at the cargo hangar. For us only left to transport the load from the seaport. But I think this is the job of our friends. The FBI agents," the officer of "OSI" continued. "We need only to wait." After these words he turned to Snowden and the others, and commanded for them to prepare such act. At this moment admiral felt relief. All obligation was in others persons hands. He wanted to sit and rest waiting for the results of all operation. Kozinsky had the same feeling. They took the chairs and sat on them. And when they did that, the officer of "OSI" has given the last instructions for the agents of FBI. And then the admiral and Kozinsky only had to wait. They passed through many obstacles concerning this work so they stayed for the next etap of the whole story. Kozinsky now was aware of the importance of the moment. And wanted to concentrate on such issue. He had strong feeling to co-operate with tthese guys from Washington. And it was truth he was content, he was in the center of this affair. So, only began to think what will be next? The best thing was, they were invited to the farther work at the project "Golden Fleece". Of the investigation. He considered it in positive way. The results of their job. For the first moment everything seemed to be like chaos. Without any sense. But he was seeing some logic in that matter. The theory of relativity became, step by step more understandable. And they together, he and admiral were thinking in the same way. Yes, Albert Einstein was not wrong. Was not mistaken. He had right. According to the famous equation $E=mc^2$ the world whirls from the beginning of its existence. Kozinsky had enough time to rethink whole matter. And what about the God? He, Kozinsky felt some kind of anxiety, when he was going deeper in the matter. He was confused. And felt even fear, when he was permitting for himself to think about whole mistery concerning such theory, whole life, world and universe. He returned to his former days when he had not such problem. It was easier. Of course, he was asking himself about the sense of existence and many others things concerning for example the religion, his faith, outlook. From these considerations woke up him a little fuss. Admiral nodded for him to go together with him and the officers and get out from the office.

"We must go out Mr. Commodore," he said in delicate tone.

"Yes, I know," Kozinsky answered, also, in the same way.

After that they did what was needed to fulfil such action. The whole group, soon, was outside and near their cars. They sat in the autos and were ready to go, to SFO, San Francisco airport. The time went quickly and after fifteen minutes the whole group were on the "one zero one" motorway. And soon found at the cargo hangar at which stood the plane hercules -c 130. The machine took the fuel and was ready for flight. Now they needed to wait for the rest company with the load from the seaport. The command has been fulfilled by the other agent of FBI wich was under an obligation to prepare the transport of machine "Golden Fleece" from pier eighty. It took the time to carry it from seaport by rented lorry and arrive to the SFO. All action was in hands of these agents of FBI. The hours went quickly and the day was approaching to the end. Soon, the lorry was on the proper place after arriving to the destination. So the operation of loading the machine could be fulfilled. They made it with care and were fully aware of importance of the load. The workers of the airport made it with experience and in proper way. Of course the prisoners were transported with the same plane and were already inside of machine. Among the group transporting these prisoners were two soldiers fully armed and they kept the control over them. So with this one plane was flying fairly huge group of people. The whole operation of loading the machine came to the end and the plane was ready to fly. For them left only wait for the permission to takeoff… So they were staying on the "Charlie taxi way" at the beginning of it and waiting from control tower on the command, permission on the start. The crew made of three men were impatient for such fact. From this reason. But what they could do? Only wait. And after a fairly long time they got the permission to takeoff. So they began to taxi on the right place among the others planes making the same action. It took certain time to be ready to start. Soon they were in the air. And next flying over San Francisco Bay. Before them long flight. So, Kozinsky and Ford again began to thought over the whole matter, concerning the machine "Golden Fleece". They together did not know correctly what will be in the future. They expected to meet with President of United States and maybe with more Very Important Persons. What will be farther? Who know? They were trying to foresee it. Already there was a night. And inside the plane was semidarkness, lit slightly. Admiral stretched his legs trying to feel more comfortably. But it did not give him relief. He began feeling discomfort. After the sojourn in hotel "Nikko" this time the flight was not belonged to the pleasure. Now he thought about the meeting in White House. Yes, it became more convenient for a moment. So he was considering such event. It will be nice. That moment in his life. He will have the privilege to meet with the head of state. And it was the cause of his joy. Even for a moment, in spite of the fact he is in the plane and is carrying the inconvenience of such flight, it was all worth while to participate in whole event. Yes, for a moment he felt better. Even smiled a little. And it caused, he felt pleasure. So, he wanted only to think about it. And only about it.

CHAPTER 8

At the White House, in the Oval Office, there, gathered small group of people. The President was also in this one. He was sitting behind his famous desk, with the hands lying on it and was rubbing his forehead sporadically. He looked on the men without any impression. They all were waiting only on arrival of Ford and Kozinsky. Among the persons, in this group was one man not so tall, as the others and also was showing some kind of anxiety. For the moment everything seemed to be all right, but it was not truth. Everyone showed impatience and they were staying near the desk of President. This small man was scientist and professor from Harvard, lecturer at this famous university. At his leg stood a bag with laptop, his personal tool. Except him in this meeting were the Secretary of State, Chief of Staff and Vice-President. And they all were waiting for arrival of admiral and commodore. The time went quickly and these both was not showing. After coming to the Andrew base they changed the plane for helicopter and this fact was sent to the President message.

"They must be here already," said the President. He was impatient. "What they do over there?" he added.

"Yes, Mr. President. We need to wait. But I think everything will be all right," one of the dignitary was trying to make the atmosphere nice and pacify the tention. But of course there was the reason to be impatient. And after that have gone several minutes of silence. No one was talking. The President was still sitting behind his desk and others were standing near it. Among them, the scientist, dressed in the suit, nervously was looking on the President and next on the others men above- mentioned. The was really inconvenient moment for all of them. The group was waiting and the time seems to pull in the infinity. Every of them was looking on the own wrist-watch and were trying to be composed and at this moment rang up the telephone on the desk of President. He took the receiver and there was the message for him, the helicopter just landed outside the White House. The President was immediately content. Only for them stayed to wait for admiral and commodore. The President informed the rest of his company about this fact and they felt relief. Yes, this time was nice and all of these men were joyful. Their mood was in better state and they were curious what kind of men, the admiral and commodore are. So they, the President and the others were waiting for the presence of Ford and Kozinsky. In the Oval Office. They were led by the White House staff to it. And after a moment were on the place. The President has seen them and did not hide his joy. From such fact. Admiral and commodore, both, have been making good impression on the President and the others.

"Nice to see you Mr. admiral," said President and they each other shook hands.

Admiral also did not hide the admire for the head of the state. The same feeling had commodore. He has seeen the President only from mass media, and now could see him lively. It was great moment for him.

"I'm very happy to see you," again repeated the President, and added, "We have prepared for you and your comrade certain kind of lecture, and of course We need to consult with You the whole matter. I know you have experience in this case. But by the way, I want to present You my company…" and he in turn introduced every man gathered in Oval Office. After that he again spoke to admiral, "We need to go to "Situation Room" so, let's go."

Next the whole group went out of the Oval Office and were going downstairs to the basement to this room. Over there, stood big table with the seats. And on one of the walls were hanging huge screen. They sat on the armchairs and the lecture just began.

"I will ask Mr. Hepburn to explain some doubt what we have, concerning this whole affair…" said the President.

Above-mentioned scientist from Harvard proudly looked on these men sitting around the table and ask the service man of this room to connect his laptop with the computer of this "Situation Room," After a while everything was ready and he could begin his speech.

"Gentlemen, thank you for permission to explain you every aspect of that matter." He said slowly and was going to continue farther his explanation. "First, I must go to the past time when the whole history began. It was several years ago. One man named Frank Slessinger had an idea, how to travel in the time. Exactly saying in the time space. All is the same. He gathered a small group of scientists, in which I was, also, and we have been engaging with this project. Slessinger is the crucial character in whole history. He was the leader of our group. He was trying to prove, the travel through the time is possible," Hepburn looked on the President and the others, and saw, his words made big impression on them. Their faces expressed it. He was satisfied. And it encouraged him to continue the lecture," gentlemen, Slessinger relied his conviction on one fact. Namely, there were, the experiences about the time, in which the time was in chaos. In the past there were made some experiemces… exactly saying there was a train in which were placed the clocks. And this train was in movement, with certain speed. After the ride of this train, when it was stopped, turned out, each clock had different time. So, Slessinger came to a conclusion, the time can be like the rubber, elastic. And moreover it, the time can be cut like film tape, which has the frames, and can be, the move of the tape, stopped at each moment. The end of the frame is not noticed, because, there is not the move of any object," the scientist looked again on the President, and this one was showing some perplexity on his face. At this moment Hepburn ended again his speech and turned on his laptop. It was connected with the huge screen of television on one of the walls, of the "Situation room". And after a second appeared on the screen some picture. On it could be seen one man, during it making some movement. It looked like the work in certain room with some kind of electrical device. "That is Slessinger," said the scientist. "I will show you several photos. I have only this material." And after several seconds appeared several pictures in which was Frank Slessinger. The photos looked even good, but did not belong to the artistic works. Slessinger on it was a man with long face and had crooked nose and with the little eyes. He had a little amount of hair and was looked like small boy without any beauty. And after the show the scientist again was continuing his speech. "We had certain experience. Namely, we accelerated certain particle to the speed of light, in accelerator, and we measured her way, and after that we found out that this particle had delay on her way to achieve the speed of light. Slessinger came to a conclusion that every particle could behave in the same way. So, the movement of Universe could be in the same process. It took two years of our work, and after that the government has been taking the control over the project. And when it took place, the public of the world had found about our work and began to protest, demanded to stop the work over the machine of time…" in this place Hepburn stopped to speak for a moment, and he looked on the whole company, seeing, his words made impression on them. No one disturbed for him. So, he took the fresh air and began to continue his speech. "Gentlemen, everything will be all right, but there is some obstacle in the whole history. There is one fact concerning the Slessinger. He did not believe in existence of dinosaurs, the beginning of Universe from Big Bang and in consequence of creation of man in this long process. He did not believe in existence of Pithecanthrope, Neanderthal, Man from Cro Magnon and the whole nonsense what Darwin invented about a man. The theory of evolution. And he was giving concrete example. Namely, please imagine certain kind of computer, which has his own logical system, in which is the memory. This computer has six senses, on which we can affect, giving impulse to each of these senses. If this computer is giving signal, we are intercepting this signal and giving for one of his senses the impulse, for example to the sense of eye sight that he, the computer is seeing something. This computer has six senses; the eye sight, the sense of smell, the sense of taste, hearing, the sense of touch and sense of balance. We can affect on every of these senses. So, there is some kind of deceit. This computer will be convinced that he is in some environment and even has his body, but everything is illusion and it is made by us, and in this way we can picture the existence of some world, but everything is false. That computer will be convinced that there is the matter, but of course it is the world made by us. Iin such trick the computer will be convinced that, for example exist the matter. Such kind of this computer is the man. Slessinger maintained that first was the man and then the Universe. Not as the science claims, first the Universe and then the man. He was sure the Bible does not lie. Adam was created truly. And the beginning of man was in paradise…" after these words Hepburn made a pause looking on the President and others, and was seeing he made enormous impression on them. First was the President who broke the silence.

"This, what you said, is so incredible, but I think that it is true. This man resolved the paradox which exist through so many years. For me, you made, the stone fell from my heart. I am personally the believer and for the first time, after your words I feel the relief."

"It is not everything. Slessinger judged that in the cosmos exist two kinds of the vacuum. The first what we have is in the universe which sends through it the light and the temperature. To our eyes goes the light of the stars, but is the second kind of vacuum, which not send the light and the matter. It is ideal vacuum, and he thought this state is in the black holes. It is the example of first state in which did not exist anything. And he thought it was the beginning of God. For the first moment appeared the thought: I am. And it is the beginning of Him. And then He created the paradise, Adam and everything what we know from the Bible and Moses." said Hepburn.

Everyone in the "Situation Room" felt for the first time the relief. Each of them was under the impression. Admiral and commodore were knowing the facts several years ago, but not so profoundly as now. They did not disturb for the scientist his monologue and admiral felt even his shirt stuck to the back. First said the President.

"So, we have now exact explanation of the whole situation. Do you think this machine is really dangerous?"

"Everything is possible, I think, but I don't know how it works. I went out of the group of Slessinger before the resolving it. I think, Slessinger took the secret with himself. And I am astonished you have this problem right now again. This scientist, Silva was to the end of this project at Slessinger, and I am sure he knows everything on the subject…but by the way. The whole project named "Golden Fleece" is so called because Slessinger was thinking about travel to the ancient Greece and mythological travel of Argonauts for the golden fleece," said Hepburn.

"That is funny name," thought the President, and then said, "what we know about the place at which is created this machine?'

For the first time said the Vice-President, "we know it is created on the Bali in Indonesia. At the town, port named Singaraja. We have enough information about this place. This man, scientist named Silva gave for us many facts of the plant in which this is made."

"Where this man is kept?" said the President.

"At Joint Base Andrevs at Maryland," answered the Vice-President, "we are in the under way of investigation. Our men from "OSI" is making it in the port of San Francisco. Silva, for sure has the partners. And we want to know who they are."

"We need to act quickly," said the President and turned to the Secretary of State, "make the connection with the President of Indonesia. I want to talk with him. We must send to this port our men, the soldiers and the President in Jakarta must agree with our undertaking. What do you think?"

"I will call to the Merdeka Palace in Jakarta," answered the Secretary of State.

"I think I need to talk with him and inform him about our action. By the way, they are buying our weapon, so, I will offer them to buy it by small sum of money. He would agree with my proposition. It will be occasion for them to make such deal." Said the President.

The Secretary of State nodded, he understand this command and again the President told to the Vice-President:

"Take one of the aircraft carrier on the west coast and certain group of soldiers. Better the airborne troops."

The admiral, still was thinking about the last words of Hepburn, he was aware of the consequences to travel through the time. And he wanted to know who is behind the whole case. The whole matter was so much complicated and incomprehensible, but slowly he has been discovering inch after inch each fragment of this puzzle. In certain moment he thought about the commodore. He wanted, Kozinsky must be present at this whole operation, there on Bali, so when the whole company was leaving the "Situation Room" he approached to the Vice-President and whisper the word for him about the commodore. The Vice-President agreed with him. Yes, someone like commodore must be there. To control the whole operation and fulfil all obligation at which he was. The Viice President took aside Kozinsky and instructed him about all action concerning the travel to Bali. He was ordered to fly to San Diego, to the seaport and land on the board of the aircraft carrier. Exactly the USS Theodore Roosevelt. It was their plan. And again on the terrain of White House landed the same helicopter as before, and took Kozinsky to the Joint Base Andrevs at Maryland. Surely it will be long time journey. So, after, the saying good by to the admiral, Kozinsky was on the board of this helicopter and were flying to this base, because he wanted to know more from the OSI officers and Silva about the place of the plant on the Bali. They took off and began the long flight. Yes, it was truth, he needed to know everything about this matter. It was his obligation, and he knew, there, in this base was prepared the place for him. The accommodation. He wanted to be there as quickly as possible. To rest and take the coffee. For example. And even take the shower. To wash himself and make the same with his uniform. Yes, he needed to repose and be ready for farther action. He truly believed, they will make the things tidied. For him left only to be at that whole operation. He knew, he will be the witness in this situation. The whole brain of this operation must be someone from the army. And he supposed, they will be from airborne troops. The strike group. When he was considering all facts of this matter, the helicopter still was approaching to the base. Kozinsky tried to foresee what will be in the base, on the place where was going the investigation. He had the hope, there, the officers of OSI should know more about all case than before, when he with admiral left this base. He was sure the officers had made the progress in the interrogation of Silva and the two others men from the crew of the ship, belayed at the pier eighty. There, in the base, obviously, really was led the interrogation, as Kozinsky has been foreseeing. The officers of OSI did not give the rest for Silva and these two men. They wanted to know everything about the work of Silva on Bali. And meanwhile the flight of Kozinsky they were continuing their work. They wanted to know every detail of the plant and place in which was produced the machine of time. They pressed Silva and made him soft, so soft, he gave them enough information about this small factory. And at last everything was revealed, so, they had whole picture of this place. And could prepare the military operation profoundly. They were waiting for the arrival of commodore, and, of course prepared for him the place to stay at this base. And inform him about the progress it that case. They already were knowing all of this event, so, when at last commodore arrived to the base, the officers of OSI have been knowing everything. They could prepare the whole plan of their action. But here existed one fact. Unfavourable for whole operation. The plant lay on the territory of another state. Foreign intervention on this place? It could not exist. But this matter was left for the diplomacy. For the Secretary of State. And now they all, Kozinsky and others were waiting for the result of conversation between the two Presidents. The United States and Indonesia. When the helicopter with Kozinsky on the board, was landing in the base, in the same time was under way the conversation between these two heads of this both states. And must be mentioned it was not easy. Even the proposition of President of United States for the President of Indonesia concerning the giving of the weapon at the attracted price did not give the positive result. The President of United States simply bargained with the head of state of Indonesia. and after a long conversation he achieved his target. For the President of Indonesia, it was not easy to agree, to receive this proposition and in fact, to allow for the alien troops to operate on his territory, even if it had been attracted and it could be occasion for them and be benefit at such moment. Yes, it was advantage, for the former named Nusantara, to get this transaction. And at last the President of Indonesia agreed for the operation of US troops od the Bali. At this moment it was benefit for the two sides. And immediately the Vice-President gave the green light for the airborne troops to act, as quickly as possible. At this moment Kozinsky had led the interrogation of

Silva and needed to refresh himself. So, he take advantage for being here and more over it gave his uniform to wash and he took the occasion to sleep and rest even for the short time. So, when he was sleeping at his accommodation his clothes was washing at the base laundry, and he was himself resting. In this way had gone several hours. So, he was informed after the sleep, he can take part in the operation. He had permission and was instructed about this fact. More over his uniform was fresh and it made Kozinsky he was in best humour. Yes he needed it. When he got the message about all facts concerning the whole operation, he supposed the troops will be from US Eightieth Second Airborne Division at Fort Bragg, North Carolina. And he was not wrong in his supposition. And after these all facts he again sat to the helicopter prepared for him, and began his flight to San Diego. On the board of USS aircraft carrier Theodore Roosevelt CVN-71. Before commodore was long journey. Over the land of North America. He left the base Andrevs, the OSI officers and Silva and all the troubles behind him and began to think of the next events concerning this whole problem with the machine of time. Through his mind were running the chaoting thoughts. What will be in the farther future? He did not know. Only suppositions. He expected, there, will be better time without any problem. The whole matter needed to be resolved withouth running to use the force. But who knows what will the next days bring? He only supposed, there, will not be more obstacles. And now he was flying to San Diego where was belayed the aircraft carrier. And then the swim to Bali. Fortunately the government of Indonesia agreed to make such operation on their territory. It was positive fact of the whole history. On the face of Kozinsky appeared little smile. He knew, the commander of the ship for sure was informed about his arrival. And they wanted only to fly secure to the port exactly to the pier fourteen. At that the ship was belayed. Kozinsky did not know the admiral of this aircraft carrier. And now had the occasion to fulfil such matter. The acquaintance. He began to think what sort of a man this commander can be? He had not the slightest idea. At this moment it was not important. He will see him after arrive to San Diego. And to know him more during the travel through the Pacific. Tall, small? It does not matter. For sure experienced. And in such way the flight lasted. During the trip they had to take the fuel so the crew landed on one of unknown airbase. And it was the moment commodore could walk a little, strech and take a fresh air. Again they were in the flight during which he was trying to sleep a little and not to think over the last events. Hehelicopter with the maximum speed was already near the town and it was late hours so, they have been flying in the semidarkness. Still approaching to the destination. The machine now was over the north-east part of the town, and was flying nearer to the San Diego bay, and the USS Theodore Roosevelt aircraft carrier. They now was in the range of the radar of this ship. After several minutes they began the manoeuvre of landing on the deck of this aircraft carrier. After adequate time everything was finished and Kozinsky could get out from the machine. For him was waiting certain man sent from flag bridge.

"We are waiting for you Mr. commodore," said this man in a loud voice trying to overcome the noise made by helicopter. And next he showed the way for commodore to inside of the ship. After short time they were on the flag bridge. When Kozinsky went to it he saw several men and they all were in the navy uniforms.

"This is admiral," said again the same man, showing with hand on one of them. The admiral was looking ahead and turned to the newcoming guest.

"Nice to see you Mr. commodore. Alfred Kozinsky, is that right?" the admiral first said to him and giving his hand for the guest.

"Yes, you have right," answered Kozinsky.

"We have waited for you," said admiral and added, "surely, you are tired, so, my adjutant will show you, your cabin. Sorry, I didn't say you my name...admiral James Greene. So, I suppose you are tired, but I want to invite to my mess on the supper. How you look on that?"

"You are very nice, I will take advantage of it," answered Kozinsky and was a little astonished from the invitation of admiral.

"So, I expect you in two hours."

"I will be ready," said commodore, trying to be relaxed and foresee what will be next. But the adjutant has showed with his head to follow him and the conversation was over. Admiral returned to his previous act and commodore went out from flag bridge following the adjutant. Next they were going in the plenty corridors to the proper cabin which was destined for Kozinsky. And, at last they found the proper door of this one. Seaman has showed for Kozinsky to get inside, and that was all. After that he has gone leaving commodore in the cabin. There were one bed and at the wall small table taking from it. So, if someone wanted to use it, he could take it from the wall. This was useful, because it did not take more space in this cabin. Commodore laid his cap on it, his shoes under and began to rest on the bed at the wall. Soon he slept like a dead man. Minute after minute, in spite of the lamp was lit. He was sleeping and time has gone quickly, so he did not notice it passed – the rest, and after two hours, someone began to knock at his door. It was adjutant of admiral. Kozinsky woke when he heard this knock.

"Enter. It is open, please!" he said loudly.

The seaman opened the door and went to the cabin.

"Mr. admiral invites you to his mess," shortly he said.

"I'm ready. Thank you," answered Kozinsky. And after a while they together went through many corridors to the admiral's mess. When they stood at the door of it, the adjutant again as before, knocked and immediately was heard the voice from inside.

"Come in!"

The seaman opened the door and announced the coming of Kozinsky. After that went out and commodor was invited to inside. Admiral was waiting for him and when he saw Kozinsky, smiled a little encouraged him to step to the mess. They both were in good mood and together smiled on such meeting. Kozinsky felt relaxed and supposed they will spend nice evening. In the mess stood a table already prepared for such occasion. Only to sit down and eat. Kozinsky looked on it and thought, how nice is to be the boss of that huge ship.

"Sit at the table Mr. Commodore please." With pleasant voice invited admiral.

"You make me the pleasure sir." Kozinsky also wanted to be nice. So he sat, as the admiral showed for him and really felt the hunger.

"I want to talk with you," again said admiral and added, "I have some instructions concerning the operation, but I don't have clear vision of this situation. So Iwould like you will inform me about it. Okay?"

Kozinsky thought about all events concerning the project "Golden Fleece", and was trying to answer, as shortly as he could, for that question.

"You see, I'm from the government side at that event,"

"Mr. Kozinsky. We waiting for arrival of the "task force" troops. It is the airborne troop. From Fort Bragg, North Carolina. They are now flying with two Chinook helicopters to us."

Kozinsky now was sure. His presumption was right. He has clear picture of all operation. And from him admiral wanted to get all facts about it. So he give him shortly all what he knew. After that admiral became more stupid than before.

"Someone in the Washington fell on the head," he thought. But did not show his conviction.

"Is it possible to travel through the time?" was in his mind, the question. He looked on Kozinsky with some perplexity, but did not want to ask more about it.

"So, we need only to wait," was his reflection on the explanation of Kozinsky. He did not understand all aspects of the theory of relativity. And was trying to foresee what will be next? He knew they must wait for the results of the international talk between the two states and arriving the troops. Maybe he was a little stupid, but after a moment to his mind was coming the thought, it is possible to travel through the time. If the theory of relativity explains it. Who could believe? And before him was sitting other person, looking as if he could be in some perplexity. Greene wanted to know more about the theory, and he thought his guest will fulfil his curiosity on such subject. But this one, also, did not know more as before. So, their conversation was not nice as they have predicted. And they talk about not interesting fact, concerning only the service in the navy. By the way, it was their common topic in which they could express their knowledge. Admiral knew, he must wait for arrive of the troops, and had enough instructions from Washington how to operate in such event. He felt even some kind of prime, he could take part in this operation, and he was impatient for that reason to do it as quickly as possible. That is why he-of course was another motif, he was corious to spend the time with Kozinsky. He needed to know about that matter, as much as it was possible. But, as he was instructed everything will be in the hands of another person. The commander of the troops, which will arrive from Fort Bragg. Kozinsky played only the role of observer and keep control over the action in next time after the conquer of the plant. So, they needed only to wait and stay at this time be prepared for this arrival of the troops. As was above-mentioned they will arrive in two Chinook helicopters and admiral was obliged to prepare the place, accommodation for the troops, when they will be swim through the ocean. He had such instructions. It was his obligation. But now, he with Kozinsky relished the free time and supper during it eat with the taste the bit of good prepared fish, taking it to his mouth. The time passed quickly. And they even unexpected how quickly. It was nice evening. The conversation has been going in good mood and admiral was content, he spent a nice meeting with Kozinsky. By the way, he had not much occasion to do it. He was glad from that reason. He needed it. After several question concerning the theory if relativity, which he asked Kozinsky, they had gone through on another topics. And in such way the time of the evening passed. At the end of their conversation they felt a little tired and it was a signal to finish their meeting. Kozinsky, also, desired to rest and they shook the hands antd it was time to go to cabin. For commodore. Again the adjutant was asking to lead Kozinsky to it, and they say good by each other. So they together went trough many corridors again to this cabin, temporary accommodation for commodore. When he was in it, he lay on the berth concerning in his mind the last meeting and the conversation. His conclusion was obvious. They must do such military actiom on the Indonesia territory. And to conquer this plant. And after that in such mood fell in the sleep.

CHAPTER 9

The night went through quickly, and he even did not notice how quickly. He felt the suction in his stomach. And thought about the breakfast. He was astonished the dish was placed for him on this little table. Someone from the crew brought it to his cabin when he was in best sleeping. It was nice. He dressed quickly in his uniform and began to eat. Everything was right, but the coffee was cold. So it was the reason of his discomfort. At the time, when he was eating, he thought about the next hours. What will be in the future? Will he stay in the cabin or will go to the flag bridge? But he did not know the way to it. He was in some perplexity. After a moment he was ready to went out of his cabin. But was afraid how to find a way to it in such multiple corridors. Someone must help him. He thought. So after a while he opened the door and was astonished. One of the seamen was waiting for him at the door on the corridor.

"Nice to see you Mr. commodore. Had you pleasant sleeping? I'm here to help you to go to flag bridge." He said.

Commodore was content. Everything was prepared like in the mechanism of the watch. First of all, the order. He smiled a little and nodded on such invitation, he was ready to go. Again they went through many corridors, passage and at last had found on the proper place. Namely flag bridge. There was staying the admiral at the window looking ahead. On the deck of the aircraft carrier. He was concentrated about what is going on the board. And when Kozinsky went in, he in the first moment did not see him. Commodore stood for a while and next he cleared his throat, in this way he has been turning the attention of admiral on himself. This one turned the face from the window and looked on the commodore. He, the admiral express his surprise:

"Oh! This is you Mr. commodore, nice to see you again," he said it in pleasurable way. And approached to him. "We have a nice day and are waiting for the arrival of the two Chinook helicopters. And the troop." 'He added and showed the place near him. He wanted to talk with commodore.

"They gave the signal by radio, they are close," the admiral had said.

"What about the order from Washington to swim?" asked commodore.

"We still waiting. There is no any command and iinstructions from them, so for us stay to wait only."

Kozinsky did not answer for that information, and also, began to look through the window on the deck. Outside was a nice day, the sun was shining and over there was blue sky without any cloud. Who could have predicted what will be in the future. Now everything belong to the diplomats. The admiral and Kozinsky were waiting for the decision from White House. It was difficult moment for all included in the affair. He, Kozinsky and the admiral now were prepared for arrival of the two helicopters. And waiting peacefully on them. Commodore hadn't any more suggestions concerning their activity. And could not counsel anything for admiral. He said all what he knew for admiral. He, now was trying to foresee what will be next. The crucial moment was approaching and they were a little impatient. But what could they do? However they were trying to keep their peace, still there was difficult time to carry it. They both had the same thoughts. The admiral did not speak keeping silence, moreover. And now they were standing close each other without any word. In spite of the hum of one certain machine, on the captain's bridge, there was relatively quietly. So, the time was going slowly, and minute after minute passed without any accident. Such state for Kozinsky was a bit inconvenient, so, he became more nervous and stood impatient. Considering the admiral, he, on the contrary kept composure. And his face did not express any anxiety. He was calm. And after the short conversation with Kozinsky, still was looking on the deck. He kept his hands behind and had the chest tense. Stood as if he had swallowed the stick. In that way he expressed, he was strong and decided man, ready to defeat any problem on his way to the success. Kozinsky looked on him with admire and compared him with his first admiral, namely with Ford. They were both, the example how to make the service for the country. Haven't many people such feature. To be strong and make the decision fast. Even if there would be many obstacles. For the first moment, when someone is looking on his face, this one could make faulty conclusion. Because he had such expression of the face. Faulty and mistaking. And in fact if had not appreciate such kind of the face.

"We have a nice day," in one moment uttered Kozinsky.

"Yes that's right," the admiral answered. And after a moment added, "you could stay here if you wish. What you will be doing today?" he had said. Still looking through the window. And after a while suddenly he asked:

"Mr. Commodore. What doyou know about the theory of relativity?"

Kozinsky at the first moment was astonished by such kind of question, but then he cleared his throat and answered for the admiral, "I think it was named relative, because it explain, foresee what is the point of reference, when is many others points in the movement. And when everything is relative. It means in the movement." For the first moment Kozinsky himself was surprised, he had made such kind of appraise. He also, understood gradually this difficult theory.

"Hm…that is interesting. In my view it looks for the main point when something is in disorder."

"That is right, what you said exactly.

Again admiral stopped his asking and there was silence. Kozinsky, also, was silent and considering this last words. Admiral has right. In his speech it was so straight, and no one could express it precisely. So, this is not so much difficult to understand this theory. Einstein really was genius when he was as a young man, and fell in on the problem. Obviously, he was looking for the common point connected the people, and he had success. He achieved it. At first moment it could be difficult to understand it, but later it become comprehensible for all. For commodore and admiral it was nice to talk about this subject, considering it and conclude about the consequences concerning the travel through the time. Kozinsky knew, their talk must be in secret, and confidential so, he was not eager to say more about every detail concerning this matter. He stood near admiral through certain time and later on he asked whether someone could lead him to his cabin. But at this moment admiral received the message, the two expected helicopters now were approaching and they needed the permisssion to land on the deck of aircraft carrier. It was already midday and they got it. Everything was prepared for them to do this manoeuvre and they were seen on the sky, gradually it was last etap of their flight. And next they landed on the stern on the vessel. It was short time exactly to do such act. Kozinsky was present at this moment at the admiral on the flag bridge. So, everything was prepared for their arrival. Then the troops went out from the helicopters and were led to the places inside the aircraft carrier. One after the second, in the row was going to the inside of the vessel. And that was all. It lasted short time, so Kozinsky wanted to get out of the flag bridge, but he was stopped by the admiral to do that, because the commander of the troops was invited to meet with him and admiral on this place, the flag bridge. They needed to wait for him certain time, and after several minutes this one arrived to them. He was led by boatswain. So, they met together and Kozinsky has known the rank of this person. He was the colonel. He saluted and introduced himself. Kozinsky for the first moment did not pay attention for the name of him. It was, indeed not important, because in the future commodore will name him by the rank.

"Nice to meet you Mr. colonel," admiral shook hands with him, and next introduced Kozinsky for him. The colonel was yet, in the helmet and only left his personal rucksack in the place of his sojourn, in this ship. So, everything was best prepared for their flow. They now needed to wait for the permission from Washington.

"I was informed, someone will be waiting for us from the government, so, it is you Mr. commodore." Said the colonel. He was tall man and made the impression to be strong and decisive. "I was instructed about our operation deeply, but they informed me, you will say more on that subject."

"I don't know much of the fact concerning the destination," commodore answered and added, "Mr. admiral will say more about the land on which you will fly."

And at this moment this one interrupted:

"We have the satelite map of the place on which your people will land. For me only stayed to flow there and have the orientation among these many islands. You know we will be on the unknown area of the water."

"Yes, this is your job to transport us to be close of the land on which we must land," peacefully said colonel. "This is island and it has many rice fields, so, we can't to land on it. On the rice field."

"Yes, I understand, but I know the Chinook helicopter can stay even one metre over the ground and not touching it," said commodore. "So, your people can make operation even in this condition. Of course there must not be the trees." He again said. And later added, "I know already there are not the trees in this place. So, I suppose you can do the landing immediately. With surprise." Next commodore gave full information about the area of the plant where is creating the machine of time. He knew it from Silva during interrogation. Yes they supposed and planned the aircraft carrier must stay away from the place of their landing and then the helicopters will start from it and carry the troops to the area of landing. Commodor, admiral and colonel did not suppose any problem to do such operation. Of course Kozinsky informed them about the guard of this plant and the weapon they have. He had all this information from Silva and the two others interrogated men. End they together went to the proper room in which they could -using also, the maps, prepare the whole attack. Colonel, admiral and Kozinsky, they all were content to do that. And finished-the preparation of the strike in every detail. So, for them stayed only to wait for the decision from the government to permit for them start to flow. The temperature in this place was high, so, commodore felt a little sweat on his body, under the uniform. He thought, the admiral and colonel could feel the same inconvenience. Kozinsky was feeling the danger hung in the air, and he was aware about the consequence of working of the machine of time. He did not thought deeply on such subject, but now had opportunity to think over it profoundly. The time was going quickly and did not work for them. The action must be take right now if theywould want achieve a success. And that was a whole story. After the preparations of their strike Kozinsky wanted to rest and relax. For the first time he felt the desire to be in his cabin and lie in the bunk. The rest of the company needed the same. it was good working day for them. Very hard working day. And they needed the prize. But one thing was inconvenient. They must stay and wait for the order from Washington. And the message was not coming. And for that reason they became more and more impatient. In that way passed long time, they began even to worry about the efficacy of their operation. They waited and only waited. Kozinsky supposed the Indonesian side for sure wanted to achieve most from this occasion and wanted to strike a bargain best as they can. But for the American side it was most important to get the permission to operate on the Indonesia's territory, only with their own force, and resolve the problem by themself. It was truly difficult moment to reach the agreement and not make big fuss around it. So, everybody were waiting for the results of the talk. Kozinsky at this moment was in his cabin lying on the bunk, and considering all facts of his past. Indeed he was tired and wanted to collect everything entirely, which he was passing in the former time. Exactly this closer events. It was hard to do such thing, because he felt confusion on his mind. Trying to be calm and concentrate on these things. He wanted to be in more joyful mood. It will be nice to think about his last sojourn in the hotel and meeting with this beautiful woman. He thought, he had not chances to realize his will and really was dissatisfied these thing did not went according to his hope.

"Don't worry about it," he thought himself, "in the future will be more occasion to fulfil such meeting, "was his last conclusion. Lying on the bed he tried to spend the moments of this time more comfortable and tried to think about the next days. The dreams snached him so quickly, he did not even feel the moment of these ones. So, he slept for good. The convenient fact was, he was alone in the cabin. And no one could disturb his sleep. Lying on the bunk, he had not any obstacles to do it. And at this moment became dark and the day came closer to the end. Trying to sum up it was waste time. Needless to say boring day. However Kozinsky felt good himself. He was preparing to spend it nice, but nothing was so good to do it. And the same feeling was in the minds of colonel and admiral. They, also felt in such mood. And only positive thing was, they served as good as their duty demanded it. The night came and next shift began. In the life of this ship. When one person is going to repose, other is taking his position. It is normal fact. To do such thing. In continuation of existence of each of ships. So, colonel, admiral and commodore now were doing the same thing. They slept. And no one interrupts in this order. This is the usual way of function of this ship. These three men now had the rest after which they must be ready to serve for their country. And that is okay. Anyone gets what he wants. Commodore got the mission. He must be content. And than it is all right. But they did not expect the things, in the future will go not according with their will. They needed to reach the success, it was obvious, but in real life there are so many obstacles, the success become illusion. And the result was going other way. Not as they wish like the order in the army. Or navy. It is simple fact. So after their night, when they were after awakening, to them came the joyful message. They got the permit to flow and start the action. The talking led by the men in Washington was positive. They achieved their expectation. The Indonisian government gave the permission for them to operate on the waters of their country. When Kozinsky got this message he was joyful. In the same mood was the rest of the company. Namely the admiral and colonel. It was like in the movie. Good movie. So, they were staying in the flag bridge together and waiting for move from San Diego. From their base. From the berth. Everybody were waiting for the end of this act. And everything went smoothly. Slowly the whole vessel began to move from the berth, and gradually flow off the pier fourteenth. They began their manoeuvre to leave the San Diego Bay. On the right they passed the USS Midway museum, and then turned on the left they were in the North San Diego bay having on the right side the airport of San Diego. Slowly they began to approach to the last etap of their sojourn on the waters of San Diego namely to the Zunga point. After certain time they were leaving the entrance to the bay, and accelerated to be at the beginning of their flow through the Pacific Ocean. The destination was the island Bali. The admiral smiled a little after the manoeuvre of flowing from the bay. It was led smoothly without any obstacles. Nothing could disturb their plan. To do it adequately, as it was in many times. The colonel returned to his soldiers leaving the flag bridge, and after certain time he was in the hangar bay, where they were placed. In one corner of this hangar, there was empty space in which they could stay. With their equipment and weapon. Everything was prepared. They were knowing all about their future action. Their strike. It was, rather, enough big group. Over the forty men. And they were aware of the potential danger. From the satelite photos they have seen the place on which they will land. The plan of conquering this object was simple. The helicopters will fly over the plant and the troops will lower on the lines to the center of this factory. They predicted, the action will be quick and perhaps without any shooting. They were prepared for such event. How to cope with this kind of operation. And at this time, when they were staying in this hangar, they were occupying with their personal doing. They were trying to be calm and, only, to stay in their space, made for them. They did not walk in the inside of this aircraft carrier. The colonel was with them all the time. To keep the control and was trying to give, to cheer up them. They were his team. Best prepared men from many others. Chosen among this kind of soldiers. Although, there was not any war time, they were calculating themself with such fact, which this time appeared. They, also calculated about the using of weapon. Maybe even the wounded men. So, it was hard to predict what will happen on the place of their operation. They calculated on the surprise attack. From the air. And trying not to spoil anything. But now they were lying on the many mattress and considering their own personal thoughts. In spite of the noise in this hangar some of them were sleeping. Or, trying to do it. In that way passed the day. The night was approaching and they had the opportunity to see the starlight on the sky. It was hot, so some of the soldiers were staying at the board and looked on the ocean and horizon. The ship was doing thirty knots per hour. His four screws were working at full tilt. In this moment it was nice to stay at the board and admire the Pacific. The same mood was shared, also, for the commodore. He did not sleep. He found the way to go on the deck so, he could, in every moment to go back to his cabin. The last episode in his life made strong impression on him. Now, he thought about it. Namely the travel through the time. Is it possible to do it? How to understand the theory of relativity? If someone had did it what would be the consequences of such act? For example travelling to the past. Someone could change the history of the world. And what about the responsibility? The history of the world would go in different way. The facts of life would immediately have changed in the history. But, for example, he, had remembered the past, and did not notice any possible change in the course of the past. There, on his mind, he should remember some other fact, as strongly as he remembers the existing. And, where is the priority in this matter? Again he thought about that woman, he met in the hotel. It was nice to think about her. She was so beautiful, so it was worth to remind of her pretty face. Indeed it was worth. The reminiscence was so vivid, so, he felt nice moment, when it was on his mind. Fresh and cold air made him conscious, and he returned to the reality. He was now staying on the deck and did not know what to do. Everything became relative. In his mind still sounded the words of Hepburn. "We have two kind of space, vacuum. One, which sends the light and matter is still existent, for example the vacuum of the Universe. And second which does not send the matter and even the light. It is clear nothing, and we have the example of the Black Hole. The gravitation in one moment must end, finish. Because everything has its own end." It was rolling in his head and again the statement, "We have scrap," concerning the computers. The human being thinks in another way than does the computer. Commodore had emptiness in his head. Many unresolved questions. Without answer. He was staying now on the deck with these words still sounded on his mind. He looked around. There were several persons from the crew of aircraft carrier. And on the deck there, stood several jet fighters. For him it was nice moment, when he looked on them. It was enormous impression on him. Still, there was the life of the ship. And it was interesting. To look on it. But at this moment, there weren't the flights of the planes. Only could be feeling some kind of calmness. And it was midnight, so, for that reason there was this little movement of the crew. He stood near the island of the aircraft carrier. And saw the action of these men. They made their practical, trained deed around these placed planes. And it was all. Kozinsky looked on them through the short time without any special motivation, only looked at them and their work. But, it was not so interesting, and after a moment he decided to go back to his cabin. It was, as usually, a normal habit on the deck. Their work. And they, the crew, have been working according to the rule around the planes. Concentrating on the job. So it was little movement on the deck. Each night and day as usually they did the same. The ship must functions thanks to their work. Exist in such way. But for commodore it became not so important tosee what they were doing. And he, for this sake, went to inside of the ship. To his cabin and berth. To rest over there. He decided not to think about the theory, but it was stronger than he wanted. And after the enter to cabin, it was still absorbing his mind.

"How they can do that?" was his thought, "to travel through the time." And next were many questions concerning the theory. He has been defying to think over it, but when he wanted to stop think about it, it stronger was coming on his mind, disturbing the calmness of his mood. Yes, it was strong. Many not explained thoughts. And moreover it became nice. To understand the secret of the life. It was pleasurable to think about it. "What this Einstein discovered?" he continued, and he was trying to understand the equation "energy equals, the matter times the speed of light to square". "Is it the equation on the atomic bomb?" rushed through his mind. "And what about the machine "Golden Fleece"?" passed next. "Yes, it can be dangerous," he concluded. And now they are flowing to the place of potencial danger. The aircraft carrier was still approaching to the destination, to the equator. Four screws were giving for it to flow at full speed even with thirty knots. The maximum speed at which the ship could flow quickly to the place they needed to achieve. Trying to be there, as quickly as possible. The nuclear reactor was giving it, and they flowed at this speed. But now they were long distance from the waters of Indonesia. For the admiral, the President of United State gave instruction to be the immediately. Don't make any exercise, only to be as quickly as possible over there. Everyone, included in this matter wanted to finish this event with all effort they can do. The time did not work for them. Every hour and even minute was important. So, it was the reason they have been hurrying. This fact was not convenient for all of them. But they did it according to the order. The plan was simple. The ship must to stop the flow at the certain distance from the Bali, not be seen from any island, and afterwards allow for the troops to fly to the place were was this plant. The rest belonged to them, to operate over there. It was their job. Trying to achieve the success. So, on the deck stood two Boeing CH-47 Chinook helicopters waiting to the usage. The weather at this time was good through the whole night, but no any soldier went out on the fresh air. Because one wall of the hangar bay had two exits needed for taking the load to the aircraft carrier. And this air was even tormenting them causing, the inside was cold. This was inconvenient for them and disturbed in their sleep. During the time of the night. Of course the colonel was with them and, also felt the same feeling. No one has ever known what will be in the future. They expected the most dangerous event. Even the death among them. And they were calculating with it. But it was their job. To stay on the guard of peace. Trying to keep control in the world. Everything among them was ordered and prepared for the action. Some of them was trying to sleep. But as above-mentioned the two exits, for the load, allow for the air to penetrating to the inside and made hard to sleep for them. During the whole sojourn of the troop in this hangar. Only they must stay in such way and waiting for the end of their journey. To be on the waters of Indonesia... And then near Bali. Who could predict what will be next? Every soldier considered on his mind even the worst scenario. According to the explanation of Silva and the two others men, the guard had the gun to keep control over it. This was their job to fulfil such obligation. Everything was in best order. And they keep an eye, on it, if someone wanted to see, what is happening in this plant. For the potential spectator outside. The plant had huge area, and everything was enclosed, even with the wire, and only with one gate leading to the inside of this factory. The person, which was the boss, controlling the work in this place, also kept everything what was important considering their work. The colonel was informed about everything what they could meet in it. Silve gave this information in best detail, so, the troop and their commandant had enough instructions, what they could meet over there. And they had, also, the view from satelite, the photos, which were helpful in their operation. They had already prepared plan, how to act, in this place. It were outskirts of Singaraja port. As above mentioned. They were prepared best, act quickly and with success. What will be there, after their landing, in the future, no one could foresee. The colonel calculated, there can be the wounded persons. On his side and the guard. And he, and his soldiers did not predict, there will be surprise. On this place. In the near future. They supposed everything will be okay. But at this time they stayed in the hangar bay, only clean their weapon. Keeping composure and looking on the crew of this aircraft carrier, which was making their job around the jet fighters. The object was the equator. And Indonesia. Former named "Nusantara". They needed to flow through the whole Pacific on the south-west of it, where was the island state. Now they had the permission to flow inside this countryAnd make their work. It was the purpose of them. So, during their journey, they-the troop was occupying, only by not so impotant things. For example to read the comic books, if someone had kept it. And it was the opportunity to think about, for example the families. If someone had it. This was the moment to rest after the exercise on the military testing ground. And the time to repose, after practice their skill, to be ready at every moment to act quickly in every part of the world. To be best in their profession. All of them were using their ability to improve the skills, and to be useful at every time, at every conflict on the Earth. Trying to counter-attack in each military event. It was their duty. So, also, this time it was the occasion to examine, how useful they were. Knowing their profession inch after inch. To be worth of their name, which they carried. Needless to say they were brave. And proud of this name. Namely-US Eighty Second Airborne Division

Fort Bragg North Carolina. And it was truth. They were best. Best prepared men to such kind of operations. So, now they were making not so important things. Waiting and only waiting for the action in the nearer future. During their sojourn in this ship, they could only test how – for example, to assemble the weapon, as quickly, as possible. And, as above-mentioned, only wait. So, their mood was not so nice. The time was boring without any interesting event. Only looking on the crew of the aircraft carrier, for example, and their work. The same feeling had the commodore. He was in his cabin, and thought about, not so interesting things. Only lying on his berth and recollected last events. He again considered all facts of the whole affair, trying -as the soldiers made to think positively about it.

"I want to be home, and not to take part in this job," passed through his mind, "it is not nice to be here. I must to control the soldiers. They could destroy something, and what to do now?" it was not pleasant, and moreover he felt boring at this time, exactly looking blankly about the future. So, he was really in not so good mood trying next to think about all affair in better way and not to be gloomy. But it was not simple to pacify and bad thoughts returned again hin his mind. He tried to think about nice moment of his life. The past. And after a while of the meeting with these woman in the hotel.

"She was beautiful, really." He sighed at the moment when he thought about her. "Pleasant face. But I had not chance to interest her about me." And again returned the moments of their stay, with the admiral together in the hotel. "What he is doing now?" was his reflection concerning the admiral. But it was all what he could do to think in bettter way about whole matter. And all fact connecting with this problem. With the project "Golden Fleece". This affair did not give him peace of his mind. And returned as the obstinate fly. So he again began to think about the attack of the soldiers. "I must fly with them in the first moment and to keep control over the whole oparation," he concentrated on the facts of their action. Yes, it was not nice moment to think of the future. And now he still was lying in the berth, nervously moving and constantly thinking over the same problem.

"And how to transport the whole equipment after the conquering the place? he worried about the whole matter. "It will not be easy to do it." Was his concern. He now was trying to foresee what to do next." It is good, the admiral asked him to be at the affair, to be present at it and to keep control over the whole matter. "Maybe my uniform is not adequate for this event, but what I will do?" Passed the thought through his mind. He now was trying not to make any problem only to give all things for the colonel and his troop. He sighed again and felt himself tired, so at this moment decided to sleep may be even for a moment. This time the dream came quickly and he after all boring thinking fell in it. This time it was easy to make it possible and without any trouble. He slept not so nicely and all facts concerning the last events made their consequences. The past, and also the future was not looking pleasant and made him to think gloomy and sad. But he was even so happy not to make the attack. It was in the hands of the troop. And in that way passed the whole night. The next were the same. Without any significant event. And these were the same with the days. Not any important facts. It was boring for Kozinsky and the troop. They were meeting together occasionally and Kozinsky sometimes met with the admiral at the helm of the aircraft carrier and colonel. So, they systematically were approaching to their destination. The waters of Indonesia became closer and closer. The crew if the ship did not make much exercise, because on the stern of it were placed these two helicopters. After these several days they approached to the aim. They were on the waters of Indonesia. And when they were in the territory of it, the admiral again ordered to connect with the headquarters in the USA to confirm the permission to flow farther in It. He want to be fully informed by them to get this permission. And the answer was good, they could to flow to the Makassar Strait, between the island Borneo and Sulawesi It was ths one way to approach to the island Bali. After a several minutes they got it by the radio and began to flow in the strait. It is long strait. It has in the shortest point one hundred and twenty kilometres width. And when they were several hours of flow, on the horizon appeared certain ship. It was destroyer. It could be seen far, far and away. The observers of aircraft carrier quickly have seen him. And it was obvious it was the ship of Indonesia. The warship. It followed them. But did not give any information for them about itself. By the radio. Only keeping the silence and distance. And they together flowed through the whole way over seven hundred kilometres, through the whole length of this strait. To the Bali Sea. It was their aim. They were approaching to this island from the north. It took for them two days to be at the point, where they could anchor. The admiral ordered to place the aircraft carrier more to the east, because he wanted to be invisible for the others ships. These waters are frequently used by many others ships. At this moment there was no any others ships. On the horizon. So they could begin to start. The weather was good, and useful for such manoeuvre. The colonel gave the command for his soldiers to gather, prepare and they one after the other went out of the hangar bay to the deck and take place in the Chinook helicopters. The day just began and everything was visible correctly. It must be mentioned, they were constantly informed by headquarters about the situation in the destination. They can get this information from the satelite photos. But no one was seen from the pictures. Everything seems to act as previosly. No one, over there, expect of this attack. When the troop was on the deck they quickly took place inside these machines. And after a moment the engines of these helicopters began to work. It was time to fly. So, when the rotor were at full force and the speed the machine took off from the deck of "Theodore Rosevelt". They began their fly. And action. To fly as the crow flies. And they were in the air... They felt, the soldiers, mixed feelings, but deep in their souls they had the will to fight. The helicopters quickly flew off and after several minutes were not visible. The commodore, who was staying on the deck and observing this takeoff, has looked in the air until they disappeared on the horizon. Now, they-the helicopters were flying over the waters of Bali Sea to the island. It did not last long time, when they saw the coast of the island. The crew has seen before them the Singaraya port. And quickly were over the Sentral Hotel. Still flying high to the outskirts on the south of the port. And than, after a certain time they were over the knowing point. In the center of the plant there was a large space, and they knew it from explanation of Silva. It was empty area and they made it the place in which they could land. The back hatch opened and the troop on the line began to go down keeping the rope. It was usual manoeuvre they practiced, so it went smoothly when they felt the ground. Still the helicopter was keeping the own position in the air, and the soldiers, one after the other could lower to the ground. It was difficult moment for the pilot of this machine to keep it in the proper high. To make possible for the troop to land and make their work. It was surprise, no one disturbed for them to do it. They landed quickly one after the others, and occupied their position. When last soldier was on the ground, the second helicopter repeated the same act. Everything was going smoothly and without any obstacle. It was surprise. There was any shot. The soldiers run in every direction and took their position. They knew what to do, because they were informed about the plan of this little plant. After the landing the helicopters flew away, and the action was continued. Everyone was prepared for the fight, and they were surprised there were not any man. It was queer, but there was not any soul. They were beginning to concentrate on the fight between them and the guard of this plant, but whole area was without any man. So, the soldiers were searching each building and was surprised, all around them was empty. Abandoned. They were astonished. There were no one. The door to each building was opened and any alive human being. The gate to this plant was also opened. And everything evented without any shot. So, they sent the message to the aircraft carrier about this queer situation by the radio, and they all were nicely surprised it went so smoothly. the plant was empty. And even withouth any equipment. Only empty buildings. And everything was showing, the staff of this plant evacuated all in quick way. It was visible. When the commodore got this message, he had mixed thoughts. One was, he was content, there was not any shot and fight, and the second what to to with this fact.

"What to do now?" he thought.

The same feeling was visible on the face of admiral. They both felt consternation. Now, it was needed to make some decision. What to do next? And for them appeared the thought. Where is the equipment?

"We have a problem," broke the silence commodore. He looked on the admiral and saw this one was, also worried. They had the possibility to keep contact with the colonel, over there. So, they together were considering to investigating all facts about this vanished things. Someone, it was clear, foresaw the event like this one. But, there is the question where is now the whole things? From this plant. Who is blamed for it? Where to looking for? Commodore and admiral could not believe. their own ears. Kozinsky rubbed his neck.

"I must go there and look on it," he said, "but one thing is positive. We have not the bloodshed." He added.

"Yes, that is truth," anwered admiral, "you must fly to them and to see what has happened over there." Was the last conclusion of admiral.

The helicopters were returned to the aircraft carrier, and Kozinsky began to prepare to the flight. Yes, all it was queer. They rack their brains. What has happened over there in the past? Before their arrival. And action. After half an hour the helicopters were appeared on the sky. And were seen in the air. Again they began to land on the deck. Kozinsky was staying with the admiral at the helm post.

"I must go," he saluted and turned on the heel to the back. After a moment he was on the deck. One of the helicopters was still ready to fly, and landed there on the stern to take Kozinsky. He quickly went in it by the back hatch and took the place. Again the machine tore off the deck and began the flight. Everything was going smoothly and without any obstacle. The noise inside the helicopter was so big, and disturbed for commodore to collect the thoughts. It was like the music led through the amplifier. Irritable. But it lasted not so long, and after a half an hour they were at the place. Near the plant, there was a piece of space, enough so big to the landing of machine as the Chinook for example. It was convenient, because the commodore will not become lower as the soldiers landed. And he went out of helicopter to this place. Around him was so many green environment, it made impression on him. After the sojourn in the aircraft carrier. Near he saw the plant Tthrough the palm. It was nice view for him. But he could not relish of it, because one soldier was waiting for him, to lead him to the plant. So, he after the getting out from the machine went with this one to the place where, was placed the plant. After a moment he was at the gate of this one. He saw it was open widely. To him approached the colonel.

"You see what has happened," this one told him, "here is no one any soul. They did the evacuating before us. But I did not know how it happened… I don't know."

"We must check everything. It is very important." It was the reflection of commodore, only. And after that words he went in one of the building. He saw, everything was taken. Only on the floor was mess of much papers. Now, the decision belong to him what to do farther. But he did not expect they will find some information about the destination. He, and the others proceeded according to the instructions from Silva, and here was not any mistake, they were in wrong place. But everything was showing, the unknown owner acted quicker than they were doing. The first thought of Kozinsky was, there must be certain spy in their company, but later he concluded, they did to much faults in their job.

"What can we do now?" asked the colonel.

"I suppose we will not find, what we looking for.," answered Kozinsky. "We did mistake and now can not do more. We can't go to the territory of Bali and search it. I must inform the White House about our discovery. The decision belongs to them. We did not find what we were looking for. And not stay here for next hours. I think, the searching of the place will carry any information what to do more."

"Do we pick up from this place?" asked the colonel.

"We will sray here for several hours and look around. Maybe there is something interesting left by them."

"Yes, sure. I will urge my boys to scrutinize this place. Who know? Maybe there is something, some trail, what they did here?" again the colonel said to Kozinsky. And after that, he went off from the commodore, to his soldiers to give the order. They began to look into every open door and the buildings to see if there is some proof, some evidence to know what has happened here. For Kozinsky it was obvious, someone in the port of San Francisco has been seeing their doing around the ship on which Silva and the load flowed from Bali. He also began to look around.

"We have not time to scrutinize this place and find something interesting us, for longer time. We are on Indonisian territory and have not permission to stay here more." He thought, when he was going through the place of this plant, "sure, they did not leave any trail, where they have gone," was his conclusion. We must pick up from here." He ended to think about all facts, considering their stay in this little factory. After a moment, when he was looking around, he concluded, there was best thing to finish their operation and fly back to the aircraft carrier.

"We have not anything," approached to him the colonel, "we must go from here," he added.

"Yes. I agree with you," Kozinsky answered.

"They needed to go out very quickly," colonel said after short time, "everything shows they made the evacuation very fast…" at this moment, when he was speaking, for the commodore came in one thought.

"Order for your people to gather all these papers, garbage. Maybe we will find some information in it."

"Yes, sure. You have right. Later we will look through it, and I have hope we will find something. "So, as he said, he ordered for his boys to collect all papers lying on the floor in every room. And the soldiers were beginning to do it, looking everywhere and gather all papers, even some shred. Kozinsky supposed, maybe in this papers was-for the first glance it was not important, they will find certain trail, some information, who is behind this all project. After half an hour they ended the order of colonel and began to go to the place, where were staying the helicopters. There, among the palms was large space and over there can stay the machines. They were ready to take off this place and fly together with these papers again back to the air-craft carrier. So, when they were taking the place inside the machines, they kept the papers with them. And even did not suppose, they were observed by someone eyes from the jungle. The whole operation lasted several hours, and they finished it after midday. So, someone has looked on them from distance. Through the binoculars. Yes, they did not suppose it. After these hours they have flown from this place, leaving it. And had only the papers as the material for their farther investigation. Maybe in this garbage is some information concerning their matter. The secret. They had hope it will be the truth. They will find something, it could show them what to do next. The helicopters took off and flew away to the aircraft carrier. Kozinsky considering all facts of their last time. He will give the garbage for the officers of OSI. To examine it by more proper person than he was. In this whole case. He thought, even now they had not the success in the investigation. Maybe in the future they will find some positive element, which could explain some doubts about whole matter. And now he was sitting with the soldiers considering their achievement. It was not so good. He did not feel well. He needed some success. Even small, but a success. It would improve his mood. What he will say for Ford, the admiral and even the President? It was difficult moment for him. During the whole process of investigation, they had only Silva and only knowledge about the creation of the machine of time. Everything has showed their opponents were best prepared for the all cases in this whole matter. He and the others did not appreciate this one, certaim and secret creator of this whole affair. Through the time of flight, back to the aircraft carrier Kozinsky thought of this matter. They now needed to return to the United States and make farther investigation. Surely, it was not easy. To find a way through the hide elements. Who is behind the whole project? During the flight to the aircraft carrier he thought about the faults they made. It was obvious there were some mistakes, they did. It was truth. They made to many faults. In the port, where was intercepted the ship must be someone from the group of people engaged in this affair.

"The officers of OSI must look for these persons over there, in the workers of port." Passed through his mind. He was seeing the faces of soldiers dimly lit inside the helicopter. He had at him the basket full of the papers gathered from the plant and was in the mood, he will have, he had such hope, the information in this garbage. Only they need to examing this all papers. TThe machine flew back to the ship and the distance with every second became smaller. He was satisfied and have this hope. They, for sure will find some trail who is behind the whole project, and owner of this plant. So he was calm and even smiled a little. The next episode of his life has gone through, and he should be prepared for the farther events. Yes, he was satisfied. He will give the all papers for the officers of OSI. That was his decision. He again smiled and was in best mood. Even if they did not find the workers of this plant, there was nice. It was without using the force against them. It was positive fact of the whole story. He again was in better humour. and in this state of mind flew back to the aircraft carrier.

CHAPTER 10

After landing on the deck of this vessel he immediately went to the admiral and related the all event, they had on the Bali. So, they this time began the manoeuvre to flow back to the United States. At this moment, he, admiral and colonel stood together at the helm post and were talking about what to do next. They needed to be there as quickly as possible. And again, as before, the same way, but this time back, they began to flow to San Diego. They left the waters of Bali Sea and began too flow to the Makassar Strait. And again through the Pacific to the west coast. After several days they were near their goal and during the journey Kozinsky went out on the deck several times to kill the time, because it was boring for him to stay in the cabin. They left the equator several days before and now were on the ocean in the middle of their journey. The weather was good and nice so, for him left only to look on the work of the crew of this vessel. And in this way has gone the whole of his trip. He had many occasion to look on the work of the crew. Sometimes it was interesting, and he, after the talk with admiral went out on the deck to observe their job. It was the addition to his boring days to see their whole activity. He was content, but not distured for them to do it. To be only the observer of the work. Yes, it was opportunity to see the soul of tis aircraft carrier. At the nice weather he had many occasion to see, how the vessel is working. It was nice to look on the sporadic fly of the jet fighter. Their flights. And he sporadically was the witness of the start of this planes. And it was interesting to see it. Several times the pointed group of the crew was gathering on the deck to go along the ship and look on the deck, if there were not left some of the elements of the jets. He had the occasion to look profoundly to the job. They were doing it with big attention to look for any parts left by the planes. Sometimes it has happening. Some parts of the jet fighters are left on the deck, so they clean the deck. It was their duty. And in such way they were doing it, because it can make the potential danger for the start of these planes. So technique was failed. And demands improving it. He was standing at the island and looked at their work. The starts of the jet fighters were so nice to see it, because he felt the force of this ones. And the noise of the planes. It was making big impression on him. When he felt enough, after such activity, he was going back to his cabin, and was thinking about the papers gathered over there in this plant on the Bali.

"What do they contain?" was his thought, but was not looking inside it, "it is the job of OSI officers.," and he, after this conclusion was going to bed. Always the same doing, during his sojourn on this aircraft carrier. It was pleasant moment to do it. And in such way lasted his return to the continent. During it he tried to be prepared for the meeting with the headquarters over there in Washington. And give the papers to them. To the staff of OSI. He was satisfied and supposed, this garbage can contain the valid information about the whole investigation. After the several days, they were at the entrance to the San Diego Bay. Commodore and the others were happy. Their way, the flow, now is ended. And their feelings were in best state. They were at home. Again they went to the bay and took the same position as before at the pier fourteenth. It was nice to see the stable land and stay on the ground. Kozinsky was feeling pleasant mood and waited for the next orders. Yes, he was happy. The matter has been continuing and he was waiting for the helicopter, it will take him to Washington. The waiting did not last long time. Everything was organized in best state. The people from White House remembered of him and of course sent the machine for him. He needed only to wait. The ship was already mooring and the crew working on the slower turnovers. At this moment Kozinsky did not wait long time for arrive of the transport. But it lasted the whole day, and the helicopter landed on the deck of this aircraft carrier at the sun set.

The commodore was surprised, it was going in such time. So, for him stayed only to go on the board of the machine with the basket of the papers took in the plant on the Bali. Yes, he was content. Everything was going in the good way. They took off and later flew in the air to the direction, the Washington. He flew in the same kind of helicopter as before. Namely the Sikorsky Black Hawk. He was tired. After many days of his sojourn on the ship and before it the flights, on the board of the others helicopters, he felt the tiredness for the sake of it. After last time he was on the utmost turnovers, and wanted to rest at any moment, it was possible. So, this time he has done the same. Only to stay on the board of this machine and only rest. It will be long journey. Through the whole land of United States. On the east coast of the state. The continent. The weather at this moment was good, so, he and the crew of the helicopter did not feel any anxiety. It will be done in the best way. Without any doubt. So, they were continuing their flight, and did not expect any obstacle. It lasted long time with the break for taking the fuel. It lasted a few hours moreover, and Kozinsky at these hours was going out of the machine to walk a little. This was the opportunity to relax and take a fresh air. And after the tank they again were starting and continuing their flight. The crew of this helicopter received the message from the White House, they must landing on the ground of it, and deliver hin and the papers to them. The President and government were waiting for him and the report from the operation on the Bali. He was informed about this order and needed only to wait, until the end of their journey. Soon, they were on the place, where stood the White House. They have landed on the ground of it, and he together with the basket of these papers had gone to the Oval Office. It was morning and the whole staff was gathered. Kozinsky, when he was inside, beginning report the whole matter.

"Mr. President everything was evacuated, and I have only the garbage in this basket. I think, in it will be some trail and I give you this one. Moreover, ther was not important than these ones. The workers from the plant did not leave any others trails. We must exaamine it ad I think the officers of OSI will find some interesting things in it."

"You had done good job Mr. Commodore. I am proud of you. The rest of the matter belongs to the OSI. I think you must rest. You did good work," was the answer of the President. And he added, "I will give you the leave from that job. We will take the papers, but you must get several days of ropose." They were pleasant words of President, and it was nice for Kozinsky to hear it. Moreover, he had some plans, when the whole matter will end, and go to New York to some of these big hotels. To rest there. It was the occasion to fulfil it. So, he left the basket for them, and only informed them about the place where he wanted to stay. The President only smiled a little on the suggestion of it and said, "we will find you everywhere. So, don't worry about the future. Go where you want."

This time, among these group of person, ther was not the admiral Ford, and commodore after this meeting with President went out of the Oval Office and decided to fly to New York. To one of the excellent hotels. He was joyful, when he thought about such occasion. Yes, it was nice to think about it. So, first thing what he was doing, was the ride to the airport of Washinton and later to fly to New York. It was simple. He shook the hands with these person in Oval Office and left them with the smile. Yes, it was nice moment. For him was waiting the car., and they after a while were on Pennsylvania Avenue. Soon, they have been finding on the road to Washington-Reagan airport And after that he was on the board of airplain Embraer -170, flying to New York. He did not some special things only seating through the whole flight. During it he again was considering all the facts of the last events. He participated. And at certain moment came the inconvenient thought. What will b

e if the officers of OSI will not find some particular things in these papers, he delivered. It will be the ending of the whole investigation. He was trying not to think in that way. And only thought about the future pleasant thing waiting for him. He had already concrete idea where to stay, there in New York. It was the Plaza Hotel. And it was the nice part of consideration of the whole thoughts on his mind. He relished for the sake of it. It was nice. And in that way lasted the whole flight. Yes, he needed the repose. And it has been making him more comfortable on the reminscence of the stay in the hotel. He will be waiting for the information from the White House. The flight came to the end. They were on the LaGuardia airport in the New York. He, at this moment concentrated on the things what he will do, to arrive to the center of the town. Must to take the taxi. He had not the luggage, so, he after the landing of the plane, when he was going out of this plane, has not been waiting for it. To take the luggage. And directly went to the post of a taxi, after the whole formalities in the airport. When he was on the place, where were waiting the taxi cabs, he took one of them and asked the taxi driver to ride to this hotel. Soon, after cover the distance from the airport to this hotel they where on the place. It was at the center of New York. The entrance to the Central Park. Five stars hotel. Kozinsky felt tiredness, and quickly wanted to be on the bed in one of the rooms. He had happiness. He got the room with the window looking on the Central Park. Because the hotel is staying at the entrance to this one. When he was in the room, he switched on the television set. And on the screen appeared two persons. After, when he took the remote control, and switched on the tv set. Again it was the one canal of the education programm, and for him seemed to be interesting. So, he paid the attention to it and made the voice stronger of this television.

"You said, there is hipothesis of existing two kind of the vacuum. One which can send through the matter and the light, and the second which does not it. But is the vacuum." It was the voice of one of the person. Commodore has heard.

"That is right. The matter does not exist in this vacuum." The second person answered.

"What does it mean?"

"We must consider, what we know about the matter. In this "Black vacuum" does not exist even the fundamental particle of matter, which we know from the examination of the matter. I think aout the examination in Cern, in the Geneva. We know, we have the knowledge about existence of the particle named "Higgsa particle", and this fundamental particle does not exist in it. The whole matter simply disappeared." And we have the hipothesis such state exist in the "Black Houls".

"Who know? maybe you have right, "was the answer of the one of persons.

Kozinsky looked on them, on the screen and was content he had switched the tv set at this moment. It interested him very strong, and he paid his attention to it, concentrating on it.

"What about, if someone will build the weapon according to this right?" he thought. And he felt needless to say a little discomfort. He felt, also, the misgiving about that fact. Yes, he and the whole company, including the President must to counter-attack to the all events. To find everyone, who was taking the part in the whole project "Golden Fleece", even the general person which was the head of the group of scientists, they were working in this project, namely Slessinger. "But how to find them all?" was his thought. Now, he must concentrate on the fact concerning his journey to the Bali. And he wanted to know what the officers of OSI will find in the garbage, he delivered. It was their job. And now, he must wait for the result of the whole operation. Everything was now, in the hands of OSI. Maybe they will find some trail, some interesting thing, it will directed them to the farther etap of their investigation. Surely it was not easy. And he felt pressure. For example, the President will be wanting some results of their work. And of course from him. At this moment the programm has ended and he switched off the tv set. There in the television was not some interesting programms, so, he wanted to have a little time to rest and not think about the fact concerning his mission. He knew, the White House will find him in proper time, when they will be knowing more on the whole matter. And after a while he was lying on the bed comfortably, did not think about the affair and taking the advantage of the stay in this five stars hotel. Okay, it was pleasure to do it. He has been waiting on the message from Washington. Did not worry of the last events, and to be relaxed from the all things, the hotel offered. He had the window, behind it he has seen the entrance to the Central Park, and the time was going nice. He looked through it with pleasure, after the get up from the bed and waited for the end of the day. Soon, it became dark, so he, lit the light in this room. For him, this evening left only to look on the programms on the tv screen. He saw the CNN show and the news on it, and was thinking, why the people have so many problems? But it was not important for him. At this moment he thought about Ford.

"What he was doing at the same time?" he wanted to be with him right now, but he knew admiral had his own agenda. It was hard to predict such fact. He had in his memory the number of the telephone to Ford, but he was not brave to make the phone call to him. He felt the respect for him. So, he threw off the thought to do it, and again lay on the bed. Still looking on the tv. He, now had the opportunity to think over the all facts of last events and make conclusion what to do next. Yes, he was fully engaged in this matter. And had always returning thought of the possibility to travel through the time. He had the same question. "Is it possible to make it?" Theoretically yes. But in the practice, he thought it is illusion. What about the disaster? The pain of the people including in the events of history. Who wants to live again in the many trouble times? And to take the suffering of the bad events. To take part in it. History of the world was not so pleasant, as someone could wish for himself. There, in it were so many conflicts.

"No. This is like some absurd, "he thought. For the first moment it looks nice, to be the witness of many historic events, facts, but after the consideration deeper it is not so nice. The fact is everyone must count with the consequences, if it will be possible. Yes, the science can make uncalculable results. If it is in irresponsible hands. So, he had enough time to consider it. And in this mood he fell in sleep. In the morning, about nine a'clock he received a message. Someone is waiting for him and wanted to meet. He agreed on it and invited that one person to his hotel room. Then it appeared, there were three persons wanting to meet. One of them was Ford and the two others the officers of OSI. He quickly prepared for the meeting. Soon, his guests were in his room. They invited together each other and began the conversation.

"You know, we have an information for you. In the garbage, you delivered, we have found certain trail. Namely the little notebook. In it is ne name of certain firm. It is the phone number. Someone has lost it. And we found it. We are here to take you to this firm, to the place we know. So, go with us." These were the words of admiral. And, when the commodore heard this, he again begin to be propared to the ride with them. It did not take long time. He was already dressed and ready to go with them. So, they together went out from the hotel room and then to the reception of the hotel to give the key cart to this one, and went outside the hotel to the car waiting for them. They knew, where to ride. Their destination was the concern of Robert Lambert. They soon were on the Broadway. The ride was not so comfortable, because the traffic at this hour. But they menaged to be on the place, as quickly as they could. One of the officers of OSI was the driver. He parked the car near the building, and they all sat out of the auto. In the brief time were in the lobby of this sky-scraper. They had not appointment and their visit was sudden. So, Lambert, when he was informed was surprised, but of course had to give permission for the entry of them to inside of the building. One of the workers was leading them to the appointed room, and said, the boss will arrive in a moment. The room was prepared exactly for such occasion. They were not waiting so long for the arrive of Lambert. He was astonished and in the bad mood. He knew, the troubles just began. With him was, of course Green. They together shook hands and first said Lambert in a nice voice:

"It is nice to see you, gentlemen, but what you want?"

"We are leading the investigation concerning some facts, but I don't say what it is. We need to ask a several question for you, "said the admiral.

Suddenly the face of Lambert became grey, but he was trying to keep composure.

"I will say everything what you want, "was the answer.

"We have information that your firm is included in certain project, namely the research over the time. Preject named "Golden Fleece". Do you know something about it?" Slowly drawled admiral.

"I don't know what you mean," answered Lambert.

"We have evidence you are the owner of some object in Indonesia. On the island Bali." Said the admital.

"I tell as before, I don't know what you mean."

"If you will not co-operate with us, we will use stronger methods against you. I promise you." These were the words of admiral. He looked on Lambert and saw this speech did not make any impression on him. So, he decided not to press him, but was trying to be nice to him after a several seconds of thinking. This was his conclusion.

"Mr. Lambert, I will give you certain time to thinking over, and if you would just have decided to tell me something, I leave for you my phone number, okay?"

Lambert did not say any words, but only took the card with the munber and gave it for Green. This one inserted it to his pocked. And that was all. Admiral, Kozinsky and the two officers of OSI, after that went out of this room and were driven to the entrance of this building. When, they were outside it, the admiral said to Kozinsky.

"We, now must to find Slessinger. I remember the address of his living. Several years ago, when we were in contact, I had the opportunity to see him in his own apartment. He was living here, in Greenwich Village, at the Grove Street. So, we must ride there. I remember where it is." Said admiral. They again sat in the car and drove to Broadway. It was best made route to achieve their destination. They drove up the Broadway, and after certain time were on the place. Admiral ordered for one of the officers, which was the driver, to ride slowly, because he wanted to remember the proper tenement house. It took several minutes, and at last they found it. It was sure, it was the exact house at which Slessinger was living. The company, after the stop, went out of the car and went up the stairs to the door. At this moment, when they wanted to go inside, certain woman was going out of this house. So, it was opportunity for admiral to ask her about Slessinger.

"Excuse me, madam! we are looking for one person. Mister Slessinger exactly. Can you give for us some information?" admiral slowly said to this woman.

That woman looked on Ford surprised and for a moment stayed with open mouth.

"This person does not living in this house... I am surprised, why are you looking for him?"

"We have some interest to this person. Do you know about, what is he?"

"I surprised; because this person has not been living here for several years…why are you looking for him?" this woman was really surprised.

"Oh…you disappointed me…"

"Maybe he now is in some psychiatric hospital"

"Why?"

"Because, when he was here living, he had some problems with psychic health," answered this woman.

"Do you know, where was he treating?"

"He said me some day it was in the "Saint Luke's Roosevelt hospital,"

"That is something concrete, "said admiral and after that they were again in the car and discuss about the situation.

"We must go to this hospital and try to find out something about Slessinger. Maybe we will be knowing about him." Admiral spoke during the ride to this hospital. Again it took certain time to arrive to this one localized at the Amsterdam Avenue. And soon, they were inside the building. At the reception they said for one of nurses, they want to speak with the director of this hospital, and they were driven to the study of this one. When, they were inside the room of the director, admiral was continuing the main role of the man who is the head of the investigation.

"I remember this man," said the director of this hospital, and added, "better will be to speak with the head of the ward, he treated this man. Go with me." He said and led them to the the study of one of the doctors. When they were going through the ward, admiral and the rest of the company saw the sick men, mentally ill, and it made big impression on them. They now, had the occasion to see the suffering of the patients. It was the man's ward and in one moment to them approched one person. Admiral looked on him and saw he had not the arms. He wanted something to say, but his speech was not understandible.

"Later John, later," in delicate way said the director, and after that admiral and others saw this patient was in strait jacket. His hands were tied behind his body, and it made impression, he had not the hands. After the words of director this patient went out and they could go to the study of the head of the ward. When they were inside the room of this doctor, admiral again was continuing the role of the head of inquiry.

"Yes, I remember this man. Slessinger," said the doctor, and after that the director of hospital left them with this one. They could talk peacefully. The doctor made impression of a man a little tired. But was nice and ready to answer every question, when admiral was asking him about Slessinger. He, the doctor was a little astonishing why they were asking him about Slessinger, but was co-operative and ready to talk.

"Why are you interesting of this man?" asked the doctor.

"We have certain reason to know about him, but I can't say why." Was the answer of admiral.

"He was the patient of our hospital and suffered on the schizophrenia,"

Admiral looked on doctor with admiration.

"He must be very patient for his ill people," he thought and after a while added, "maybe you will remind some facts concerning this man. You know, it is very important for us." Continuing admiral. "If not this time, perhaps later. I leave for you my phone number, and will be waiting, if you will remember something," these were the words of admiral.

"I, only rememer, he was fascinated about the history and facts of the French Polinesian. His dream was to live there."

"We must find him, help us,"

"I remember only that fact,"

Admiral and the others of his company were seeing the farther conversation will not bring more results, so they left the doctor and asked for showing the way to the exit for them. One man of personnel did it. And when they were outside the hospital, on the Amsterdam Avenue, in the pocket of admiral sounded the telephone. He took it to his ear and began to listen. The call was from Washington, from the White House, and exactly saying from the President. Admiral was listening for a while and when the call has finished he said:

"The President wants to see us and to talk, you and me," he showed on the commodore.

Kozinsky was a little surprised, but of course was ready to fulfil the order. So, it took enough long time. When they were in the Oval Office. And now they were standing in front of the President. He asked the question for them:

"How the inquiry is going?" he said.

"For this moment we are in deadlock. Sorry, Mr. President, but now there is not any positive fact, concerning the whole matter. We know who is behind it, but we can't do any more. We need more time. Perhaps the future will bring some proper facts. We must wait. I have some idea. To look inside the computers of one firm, which is, perhaps the sponsor of the whole project. But we need the permission, even from you to find out everything what is important." The admiral said slowly.

"You have this permission. I give it for you," impatient said President.

"So, for us left to go again to this firm and to make the order." Satisfied was the admiral.

"Do you have more information?" asked the President.

"No sir,"

"So, go there and do it," was the conclusion of President. The conversation was over, and then the admiral and Kozinsky went out from Oval Office ready to make farther inquiry. They again were on the board of plane to New York. They did not expect how proper fact is going. When they were in the airport, there again sounded his telephone. Admiral was astonished. It was the voice of Martin Green. Yes, it was a very surprised for the admiral. From Green side he wanted to see, make appointment with him.

"What is he want?" after the speech with him, admiral informed Kozinsky about that fact.

"Did he give you concrete reason for this call?" Kozinsky asked.

"He wants to meet in Central Park, and gave information where to meet."

"Where is it?"

"In the heart of the Central Park," was the last answer of admiral, "at the Bow Bridge," he added.

Next they took the yellow taxi cab and ordered for the driver to ride to the entrance of the Central Park. It took certain time to be there. And then, when they were on the proper place they sat out of the car and began to walk slowly. They did not hurry. They had the time to be there even if it will take longer time. The weather was nice and make them to be in the mood very pleasant. At last they were on the place. There were not any people, and from distance they saw Green was standing alone in the middle of that bridge. He stood there waiting nervously for them. He was excited. And when he saw them approached to him he got more nervous. Our both came to him, but not gave him the hands.

"What do you want, Mr. Green?"

"I will tell you everything. My boss, Lamert does not know about our meeting. I am here from my own decision. Yes, you had right. This whole project was begun by our concern. We met Silva and offered him the help in his troubles…"

"Where is the plant making the machine "Golden Fleece"?"

"We have second place prepared to such events as were at the last time. It is hidden in jungle. It was my idea to make it for the reason, if something like your visit will appear. And I had right, we evacuated the plant to the next place, because we had signal, you intercepted the load in the port over there, in San Francisco. That is all," Green said it peacefully.

"Why did you tell us this all?" asked admiral.

"Because I saw the hell."

CHAPTER 11

The whole matter went now very quickly. The OSI made the air ride on the firm and Lamert was in shock when the officers of this institution appeared in his firm. At the meantime admiral and commodore also not waiting and stopped their activity. On the second day of their operation admiral received the phone call from the doctor of Saint Luke's Hospital. He was surprised why he has been calling. The doctor wanted to see with him. The reason of his request had the sense. When admiral was in the room of the doctor he got the message. surprisingly. After several years of silence to him Slessinger suddenly gave the sign of his live. The doctor received the postcard from him. When admiral kept this card in his hand, he could read it came from Tahiti. On it Slessinger sent the greetings for the doctor and whole staff best wishes from this island and gave only one but very important information. He wrote it in simple way;greetings from Tahiti and Tautiry. It is possible he could live over there.

"Thank you Mr. Doctor," he said and took this postcard with him. So, for them left only to be prepared again for the voyage. The aircraft carrier "Theodor Roosevelt must to flow again in the same purpose. To the same place. Their destination again was the island Bali. The officers of OSI made their job, there in the New York in the Concern of Lambert, and admiral and commodore began to be prepared to this trip. So, they, this time together Ford and Kozinsky flew again on the deck of this vessel. The commander of "Theodor Roosevelt" was content to see again the commodore and this time also, Ford on the flag bridge.

"My name is James Greene," the commander has said giving his hand for Ford. This one made the same, and also, was content to see him.

"Mr. Kozinsky said me many of you,"

"I know about you also. Mr. Greene," answered Ford and looked on him with pleasure. After such invitation they went to the mess of admiral Green. Kozinsky was in it in the past and knew the room. It was nicely to be there. The admiral Greene also this time invited them on the supper. After a moment they relished caused by the dishes. They ate it with pleasure. And after that when they finished, by the way, during the supper they had the occasion to know each other closer. Yes, it was nice moment to take part in such meeting. For Ford the commander of this vessel seemed to be nice and even interesting man, in spite of young age. This one had only forty years of life. The time went quickly and they did not noticed, that two hours of their meeting had passed. So they were a little tired and admiral Greene was seeing, his guests needed to rest. Repose. So, he suggest them to end the meeting and ordered for the seamen to lead the guests to their before prepared cabins. For Greene stayed only again to wait for arrival the same as before, troop of airborne division, and the Boeing CH-47 Chinook helicopters. But this time they supposed, there will not be necessary to use the force. Greene has looked from the flag bridge on the deck, feeling happy. He was happy. Really. He could take part in such operation. Everything was prepared for the troop as before. But this time they-the soldiers, will get more place inside the aircraft carrier. So, they were waiting on arrive of these helicopters with the troop. It was already the night. But he knew the pilots have the skill to fly at every circumstance and can land on every difficult ground. The deck of the aircraft carrier was illuminated, to make easier for the machines to land. Soon, Greene received the message they were closer, by the radio. And he decided to stay and look until they will arrive. The weather was pleasant and without any cloud. So the conditions were proper to their neccesity. And Greene, soon saw the lights of these helicopters on the sky. He waited several minutes at the moment when they ended the landing and after it went to his mess. Now it was the time to flow.

Their destination first was the island Tahiti. Correctly saying little village Tautira. Ford had the presumption in this little village is living Slessinger. So, he had hope to find him and take back to the USA. And again, as before they were leaving the San Diego Bay and flow to the open sea. To Pacific. It was their route. After certain time they left the waters of this Bay and began to flow to the French Polinesia. On the deck was silent, and only the wind sporadically blew showing he is existing. The night was nice and with calm weather. With the thirty knots of speed, they flew to farther voyage. And at this time Kozinsky and Ford were dreaming until the morning. They will be prepared for the day, until they will finish their mission. It was their duty. The time of meeting Slessinger was approaching. And after their sleep, in the morning admiral said for Kozinsky:

"You must go to this village alone, and find there our fugitive."

Kozinsky did not say any word, but thought it will be difficult for him to fulfil such task not knowing the French. He was a little worried about such fact, but it did not disturbed his desire to make such task. He was ready to fulfil this order. And after several days they were near the island. So, the commodore prepared himself to the flight on the island and to land near the village. They had the full information about the topography of the island. They had it from the satellite photos. He and the two others soldiers were prepared to went on the board of one of the helicopters, they started and flew in the direction of the island. The machine has flown over the heads of the inhabitants and made the attraction for them. And then making huge circle landed on the dark sand beach. After a moment they went out of the machine and next had gone to the houses of the village standing among the palms. As usually this landing was big fun for the children. But even the grown-ups people were astonished.

"What do they do, here in our village?" seems to be questioned.

Commodore went farther to the land and the two soldiers followed him. When they were in the village Kozinsky had a little trouble.

"How to find this scientist among this many people and houses?" he asked himself. But later had idea to ask the children simply saing the name of Slessinger. And they quickly answered for his question.

"Monsieur Slessinger?ici," answered this group of kids and showed the way with their hands. Kozinsky and that two soldiers follow them and in a moment were at the house of the scientist. Kozinsky did not expect the matter, the looking for him will be in such short time and success. He now was standing at the entrance to this house. The door were open and he ordered for the soldiers to stay outside, and knocked to the wood frame of the door. After a moment someone went out to him. Yes this person was Slessinger.

"What do you want?" he asked.

"Mr. Slessinger I suppose?" answered and asked the commodore.

"Yes,"

"My name is Alfred Kozinsky. I am commodore and we are here to take you to America."

"Why? What I did? I don't understand."

"You are the scientist, you worked on the project "Golden Fleece", and we must take you to Washinton to ask you certain questions."

"Why? Why you will not leave me now?" and after that added, "I want to live peacefully and don't want any connection with you,"

"I have the order to take you,"

At this moment Kozinsky felt like interloper going in certain person live with the shoes. And Slessinger also felt the same. It was dirty job After a while Slessinger saw his arguments did not work positively. So, he said to commodore;

"Please, wait a moment. I will take the dress. You see I am in the gown. And I must go to the second room to take it. So, when he said it, he approached to the door of this room, he opened it and in this moment from that room appeared the huge light. Slessinger went into it and gradually beginning disappear. Commodore could not look on that light. His heart was beating so strong and this all unusual view made him like coward and he, at the whole time, when he looked on the disappeared figure of Slessinger, felt enormous fear. He turned back quickly and run off the house. He hit the little china sculpture of Budda, which fell down on the floor but not broke from the table. Next he passed these two soldiers, they also were astonished, and run like mad man to the beach. When he was there he felt, his legs were like from rubber, he fell down on his knees and began to cry. Like little child. And suddenly before his eyes unseen finger on the sand began towrite. E=mc².

THE END